FREE FALL

"There isn't even static," Ellen said. "The receiver's not working ... Try the transmitter again."

"Mayday. Mayday. This is capsule nine-eight-four. Our receiver is not working. We cannot hear your reply. Please come help us. Mayday."

... Kevin felt a knot of fear in his stomach. Trapped in an orbiting steel coffin ...

"We'll have to disconnect from the capsule air supply before we can open the hatch," Ellen said. "If the hatch will open at all—" ...

The capsule hatch wouldn't open until the air was gone. There'd be no point in pulling on it; at seven pounds a square inch, hundreds of tons of air pressure held that hatch closed. They couldn't open the hatch, and they had less than an hour of air.

"I never thought they'd do it this way," Ellen said.

EXILES
TO
GLORY

JERRY POURNELLE

ace books

A Division of Charter Communications Inc.
A GROSSET & DUNLAP COMPANY
360 Park Avenue South
New York, New York 10010

EXILES TO GLORY

This novel originally appeared in the
September 1977 and October 1977 issues of
Galaxy Magazine, Copyright ©1977 by
UPD Publishing Corporation, Inc.

An ACE Book

Cover art by Boris

First Ace Printing: July 1978

Printed in U.S.A.

For Dan Alderson, the sane genius.

CERES

Asteroid at average distance 257 million miles (2.767 AU) from Sun.
Mass: 8 X 10^{23} grams. Radius: 370 kilometers.
Surface area: somewhat larger than the state of Texas.
Period: 4.6 years. Rotation: 9 hours, 5 minutes.
Surface gravity: 38.9 centimeters/second = .04 Earth gravity.
Escape Velocity: 5.37 X 10^4 centimeters.
Path velocity in orbit: 17.9 kilometers/second.

Largely composed of stone, Ceres has an easily accessible metallic core containing rich, commercially valuable deposits of gold, silver, tin, copper, nickel, and iron, as well as super-heavy elements such as Arthurium in recoverable quantities. Water-ice exists both in permafrost and underground deposits.

The first expedition to Ceres in 1997 was financed by Hansen Enterprises (Ltd. et Cie, General Headquarters Luna). Interplanet of Zurich subsequently made extensive investments in mining and refinery operations on Ceres. The commercial future of this venture is uncertain.

I

FIRST HE HEARD THE CLICK of the switchblade. Then the whining, feral voice. "Hey man, gimme money!"

There were four of them in his path: two slouching against the wall, two erect and staring. Westwood was deserted. The UCLA campus beyond showed lights, but it might have been in another city for all the good it did him. Kevin tasted sour bile, felt the sharp knot of fear in his stomach. They moved closer.

"Come on, hand it over, you sumbich." The spokesman's blade moved in intricate, blurringly fast passes inches from Kevin's face. It gleamed dully despite the powersaving partial blackout in the city. The blade's wielder laughed as Kevin cringed away.

Kevin was a well-muscled six-footer, had played football for UCLA and made his letter in his junior year before the pressure of studies made him drop from the team; he was certain he was more than a match for any of them—for any two—but the knife seemed hungry for his eyes, and he felt only fear and shame. His legs wouldn't move. He reached into his pocket and took out his wallet.

"Watch," the mugger said. "Take it off." The

whining voice was filled with contempt and sadistic power-lust. Kevin felt it wash over him, and felt contempt for himself. "Turn out all your pockets. Deucey, rub him over."

Another of the young gangsters—they couldn't, Kevin thought, be more than sixteen—came up behind him and rubbed his hands over Kevin's clothes. The hands moved insultingly, paused in insulting places, then reached into his pockets and took out his lighter. "Aw, he's got cigarettes," Deucey said.

'Good for you, mother," the spokesman said. "We cut you if you don't have cigarettes. Cut you good. Now we miss the fun. Get in there." The knife jerked to indicate a dark alleyway.

Kevin was beyond terror. He had never experienced the feeling before, but he recognized it now, like something known previously from a faded photograph. They pushed him off the street and away from his last hope of rescue. The street lights dimmed even more just as they entered the alley; it was almost pitch black in the stinking passageway between buildings. His foot kicked something, trash or a dead cat, and insanely he thought of the city garbage strike—would anyone find him for weeks? He was certain the gangsters were going to kill him, and kept worrying about that: would the strike end in time for them to find his body?

Suddenly he was surrounded by the smell of naptha, strong enough to overpower the smells of urine and decay in the alley. He felt a chill on scalp and shoulders. Lighter fluid. They were going to burn him alive!

Desperation drove him forward, away from his captors for a moment. The knife had terrified him, but the threat of becoming a living torch did something else. He was no less afraid—more so if that were possible—but now there was rage and hatred as well. He cast about for a weapon, anything to defend himself. He was certain he was going to die, but now he wanted to take them with him, to end this humiliation and show them he was a man—

His hand struck a garbage can. It had a lid, and he seized that by the handle. Years before, when he was only seventeen—it was only five years ago, but at this moment it felt like two lifetimes—he had participated in a tournament held by the Society for Creative Anachronism. The SCA fighters used wooden swords, but their armor and other equipment had been real. He'd been fascinated by the use of shields as weapons. A hand grabbed his hair, and despair gave him strength of a different order than when he'd fought in the SCA tournament.

He swung the lid blindly, felt it clash, then swung it backhand against the spokesman's face. He felt bone crunch, and shouted his triumph.

As the first gangster screamed Kevin used the shield to deflect another half-seen knife attack, then again blindly swung the lid backhand with all his strength. He couldn't see anything, but he could feel when he connected, and he wanted to hurt them. He hated them with all his soul, and he wanted them to feel as humiliated as he had felt. He struck out again and again, felt the improvised shield strike home at least once more. Then he was past them and in the street.

The sight of freedom ahead robbed him of his rage; he turned and ran. Two of them followed him for a block, but they didn't have the wind to keep up.

He ran on and on, long after he could no longer hear their heel-beats behind him.

* * *

The Los Angeles policeman showing his badge at Kevin's door was big and burly, and looked as if he ought to be in uniform instead of neat civilian tunic and trousers. Kevin's landlady stood disapprovingly behind him in the hall.

"Detective Sergeant Mason," the policeman said. "May I come in?"

Kevin couldn't think of anything he had done. He was exhausted from standing in lines for his food ration stamps, and he wanted to send the policeman away, but he was afraid that his landlady would believe he was in trouble with the law. Mrs. Jeffries was a good friend to her student tenants. She would let them be late with the rent, but she didn't want police trouble in her rooming house. "What's it about?" Kevin asked. His voice sounded much more calm than he felt.

"This yours?" The policeman held up a wallet.

"Uh—"

"It's got your ID in it," the detective said. "I'm returning it. No big deal. Want to talk about how you lost it."

"Yes, sure, it's mine," Kevin said. He felt relief, and saw that Mrs Jeffries had lost her worried look. Kevin winked at her and got a slight smile in return before she left and the policeman came in.

4

The room wasn't very large. There was a couch that could make into a bed, but it was long enough for Kevin to sleep on without unfolding it, and he never opened it. The walls were lined with bookshelves. Over the years the many students who'd lived there had added to the shelving until there wasn't a bare wall. There were two desks and a table that came from the Salvation Army Thrift Store. At the opposite end from the entrance was an opening onto an alcove where a stove, refrigerator and cat litter box filled what would not have been a very large closet. The room smelled of food and cats. The desks were littered with papers, pocket calculator, library reader-screen, opened books, drafting tools, and junk mail.

"Reminds me of my student days," Sergeant Mason said. "I stayed down the street in a room just like this. What class are you?"

"Senior, I think."

"Kevin Senecal," Mason said. "Senecal. Unusual name. Don't think I ever heard it before."

"It's Norman French. We think it used to be Seneschale," Kevin told him. "That'd be Stewart in English—you know, meant Steward." He wondered why he was so nervous with this policeman. The cop had brought back his wallet, and Kevin hadn't done anything to be afraid of. But the policeman's manner was unusual, cagey, as if he were trying to think of the right way to say something unpleasant. He didn't think the policeman would have come alone if he'd intended to make an arrest, but why was he acting this way?

Kevin had never had much contact with police:

in the neighborhood where he grew up police were to be avoided. Cops didn't have much respect for poeple on welfare and unemployment. When Greg Tolland's People's Alliance won the White House and Congress that had changed for a while, but then Tolland was hounded by the press and the Alliance was smeared and things went back to politics as usual and—

His reverie was interrupted by the policeman. "Here." Mason tossed him the wallet. "Put it away. Officially, I never saw it."

"Uh?"

"Look, Kevin—you don't mind if I call you Kevin? We took this off some bad people last night. Guy carrying it had a broken jaw. His buddies were trying to get him to a doctor."

"You caught the bastards! Good work," Kevin said. He looked at the policemen with new respect. His mother, who had once had a better life, had always told him the police were all right. "But isn't the wallet evidence?"

"You don't want to prosecute."

"But—"

"No." The policeman was very firm. "Look, those guys belong to the Green Fence gang. If you identify them, you won't live until the trial. Actually, you're probably in trouble anyway; they wouldn't have kept the wallet if they didn't have something in mind. Usually they just take out the money, put the credit cards into an envelope and mail them to friends—and dump the wallet so there's no evidence if we shake them down. They kept yours. I don't have to be very smart to guess why. You did a good job on the guy with the broken jaw. And a better job on the other one."

The policeman was looking carefully at Kevin's face. Kevin didn't care. He was glad that he'd hurt those bastards.

Whatever the policeman saw seemed to please him. "You didn't know, did you?" the cop asked. "You killed one of them. That garbage can lid caught him just at the base of the skull. Clean and neat."

"Jeez—" Kevin felt a rush of shock, fear, and anger. "I never meant to kill anyone! Am I in trouble for that?"

"You would be if we knew who'd done it. But of course we don't. Never found anything at all. They must have ditched the wallet."

It took Kevin a moment to catch on. "But—"

"But nothing," Mason said. "We got ourselves a new DA, a real People's Alliance type, and we've got judges who don't approve of 'deadly force.' Somebody killed a juvenile last night, and you don't kill juvies in this town. That's bad news."

"But they were trying to kill me! They poured lighter fluid on me, to set me on fire!"

"Can you prove that?"

"How the hell could I prove—"

"Exactly," the policeman said. "You can't. And we can't do one damned thing for you, Kevin. If we give you protection the DA will want to know why, and we can't tell him or he'll have you up for manslaughter of a juvie. It gets worse. The Green Fence will be looking for you. If you're smart they won't find you."

"You're telling me I ought to run because some muggers tried to kill me and I defended myself?"

Kevin's face showed anger. His fists clenched and he felt the blood rising—

"Nope." The detective's calm was maddening. "Remember, I don't even know who you are. I'm just returning some property I found while I was off duty. Which, by the way, I am now. You got any beer in that 'frig?'

"Sure." Kevin went to the refrigerator. Snowdrop, his white kitten, was sitting guard on top of it. She mewed hopefully when Kevin opened the door, then looked resigned when no cat food or milk came out.

Mason popped the top of the beer bulb and made a face at it. "I liked this stuff in bottles or cans. Now we got biodegradable cardboard, and it don't taste the same." He drank it anyway, a long healthy glug. "Can you change apartments?"

"I'm a month behind here. There's no way I could get the money for a new place."

"Probably wouldn't help anyway. They'd follow you when you moved. What are your plans?"

"Well, I graduate this term . . . "

"You might last that long. Want some advice? Keep out of dark places. Don't have a routine. Come home at different times, and don't eat in the same place every day. Keep the shades down and keep your shadow off the shade. Lock up good when you go out. Get a better lock. Get *two* locks. And stay with people you know." Mason drank again. His lips tightened as he set the bulb on the couch arm. "Kevin, do you think I *like* this? I'm a cop. My job is protecting people. And I'm telling you that I can't protect you, that the bastards in City Hall won't let me. I don't like that much, but

8

you tell me—what should I do?"

"I don't know," Kevin said.

"Yeah. Well, if you think of something, let me know."

It seemed appropriate that the lights dimmed just then. The windmills weren't getting enough power, and it took a while to get generators fired up.

* * *

Long after the policeman left Kevin sat at his desk staring at a book. He read the same page three times, but none of it registered. He was afraid. His books said he lived in a post-industrial society and described the benefits in glowing words, but the police couldn't help him.

Out there somewhere was a gang of nameless children—the DA would call them children, and Kevin a child-murderer—and those children would kill him if they could, and the police were helpless. The United States of America in all its awful majesty was no use at all. The police could give out tickets and harass taxpayer demonstrations but they couldn't protect Kevin's life.

His life had been settled and orderly, completely planned. He would get his degree and go to work for one of the big international corporations, perhaps even go out to one of the near-Earth space industries if he could get a post. Junior engineers weren't paid very well, because nearly everyone graduated from state universities and had some kind of "professional" job—or didn't work at all —but when he got his degree Kevin would be eligible to join a strong union, and the union would keep the pay raises coming. Kevin looked forward to marriage, a house, a car, perhaps a camper and a small boat.

When he told his friends they usually laughed and said it sounded dull, but Kevin didn't mind. Dull was fine, as long as it was secure. After the years of living with his mother and his brother on welfare checks and food stamps, split pea soup, chicken once a week when they were lucky, patched clothes and shoes bought from the Salvation Army, dull-but-secure was attractive. Dull meant buying food in private stores instead of standing in long lines at the cooperatives. Dull meant living in a neighborhood where the police were polite and respectful. Dull meant all the things Kevin had never had and always wanted.

And his dream of dull security was vanishing with the memory of a garbage can lid smacking into human bone.

The book stared back at him. "The most crucial questions that will be faced by every post-industrial society will deal with education, talent, and science policy. The rapid expansion of a professional and technical class, and the increased dependence of the society on scientific manpower, suggest a new and absolutely unique dimension in social affairs: i.e., that the economic growth rate of a post-industrial society will be less dependent on money capital than on 'human capital.' "

The words blurred and the idea was silly to begin with. The most crucial question was: how would Kevin Senecal stay alive long enough to graduate and get his union card so that he could find a job?

* * *

The letter had been generated by a computer. It

10

had his name spelled 'Senegal,' but the student ID number was correct. It was for him.

It told him that two summer classes he'd taken at California State University, Northridge, were not recognized as transferable for credit to UCLA. "As these classes are prerequisite to other classes required for graduation (see schedule 4 below) you may not hold credit in the classes named in schedule 4, and thus you have not completed the requirements for graduation. Your application for graduation is denied, and your present class status is second-year, commonly called sophomore. Upon completion of the required prerequisites, and following that completion, your successful completion of the courses noted in schedule 4 (see below) you may again make application for graduation."

He read it three times. It said the same thing each time. Instead of graduating in two months, he had two more years of school. He crumpled the letter in rage, but then carefully smoothed it out. These things happened. It was futile to get excited. Computers often made mistakes. He telephoned the UCLA Appointment Exchange and registered a request to see his advisor.

They could give him one in two weeks. He raged silently at the phone, but there was no point in being angry with a computer. It could only understand a very limited vocabulary. After he hung up, he felt ashamed for being so angry. It shouldn't be surprising that it would take a while to see his advisor. There were over 100,000 students at UCLA. It took time to arrange for a human interview.

II

He took the policeman's advice: varied his schedule, stayed off streets at night, and always locked his doors. His friends didn't notice. He'd always been something of a loner and a bit of a bookworm since he dropped out of the football squad, so there was no one to miss him. The girl he'd been dating had found someone else two days before the muggers had caught him, and except for Wiley Ralston no one would care.

Wiley was a student one year ahead of Kevin, staying on after graduation to specialize in space industry technology. Engineering students were never popular on campus, and those going to space were hated. The One Earth Society, and other anti-technology groups, picketed the engineering building nearly everyday. Their lunch-time demonstrations seldom got out of hand, and Kevin had become accustomed to their shouted insults whenever he went in or came out of his classrooms. Now, though, they began to get on his nerves. When they ritually shouted "murderer!" at him, he remembered the crunch of bone that he'd felt that night in the alley.

"Hey, don't let those nuts shake you," Wiley

said as they walked past the demonstrators.

"Aw, they don't," Kevin said. They hurried toward the cafeteria. There was a long line waiting. "Not really anyway."

"You ever really listen to them?" Wiley asked.

"Once," Kevin said. "Didn't make much sense to me. They kept telling me we're wasting all that money in space when there's so much needed here, and I know better. Without space technology we'd be a lot worse off than we are now. What goes to space wouldn't help anyway. It's just not enough."

Wiley nodded, then waved at the line ahead of them. "Yeah, except sometimes I wonder."

"You?"

Wiley Ralston laughed. "Not very often. Just sometimes. Like this. Why're so many people lined up for lunch? Because you get a free lunch on your student ID card. Which is why most of these turkeys are students to begin with."

Kevin didn't say anything. It was one reason he'd decided to go to college. The state university was free, and the food at the UCLA cafeteria was better than anything his mother had ever been able to afford on straight welfare.

"Better to be a student and eat than be unemployed," Wiley said. "And hell, it's all this technology that keeps people unemployed. That's the way they see it, anyway."

"You know better," Kevin said. "What's important is production. High production means a lot to go around, and—" He stopped, because Wiley was laughing at him.

"Gotcha," his friend said. He tossed back a

shock of unruly red hair and grinned broadly.
"You know the trouble with you, old buddy? You
care. These jokers say the world's got to learn to
use low technology, be kind to the Earth, live with
the land, or our great-grandchildren will have
green tentacles or something—"

"They never—"

"And you really worry about whether they're
right or not," Wiley finished.

"But they aren't, and I can prove it—"

"So-friggin-what?" Wiley Ralston demanded.
"Look, Kev, maybe they're right. Look around
you. Food lines in the US of A. Want in the middle
of plenty. And that's here! All over the world people are breeding like mad, nobody's got enough of
anything, and hell, maybe all this space effort *will*
be the last straw, the push that makes the donkey
lie down and die. So what? You say space will save
the Earth, they say it will kill us, and I say—
somebody's going to get rich out there, and that
somebody is going to be Wiley Ralston. I'll get
mine, and if they're so stupid they'd rather put on
demonstrations than get in on a good thing, that's
their lookout."

But Wiley had spoken too loudly, and others ov-
erheard. An alternate technology group came up to
argue. A Zero-Growth group joined in, then some
fanatics from the One Earth Society. If the various
protestors hadn't got to arguing among themselves
the scene might have gotten ugly; as it was, Kevin
missed his lunch.

Even so, he preferred to be in crowds. Most of
the anti-technology students wouldn't actually

harm him. None wanted to kill him. Better them than the Green Fence.

* * *

His advisor was a prim, rather prissy-looking woman in her thirties. She reminded Kevin of a sentence in his sociology book. "The post-industrial society is organized around *knowledge*, and this gives rise to new social relationships and new structures which have to be organized politically." Ms. Rasmussen was the embodiment of that: she had *knowledge*, or was supposed to have, and that gave her power.

As he faced her, Kevin thought that was a bunch of horse puckey. She had a job that gave her power, and she liked that a lot.

"What seems to be the trouble?" she asked. She shoved a form toward him. His student ID card embossed his name and ID number on the form, but he had to fill in the address by hand. She waited until he was finished before she picked up the computer letter Kevin had handed her in response to her question.

She read it through twice. "This seems to be in order," she said.

Kevin wanted to scream at her, but he held his temper. Years of watching his mother manipulate the welfare workers had given him both patience and technique. "Please ma'am," he said. He felt sick saying it, but forced himself to keep his tone respectful. "This costs me two years of my life. It isn't fair, ma'am. I worked hard, and they tell me I'm still not through. Please, can't you do something?"

She punched buttons on her console. "I'll need your ID card," she said. She inserted the plastic into the machine. Records flowed across the screen. She peered at it, adjusting her glasses with fussy little movements, smiling thinly, a superior smile, the smile of those with power. "It's all in order," she said, "just as the letter tells you. You took the courses without the proper prerequisites, and so of course you're not entitled to credit for them."

"But, ma'am, I had the prerequisites," Kevin whined. He tried to keep his voice pleading, showing that he appreciated all that Ms. Rasmussen was doing for him. The effort made him tense. He hated himself, and suddenly realized that this was the way he'd felt when the muggers had him: helpless and violated. And he felt that way a lot, lately.

"You did not have prerequisites as recognized by this university," Miss Rasmussen said. "I'm sorry, but I can't help you." She sounded pleased. She began marking the form; it would be turned in to record that she'd had another interview. The accounting machines needed the completed form to justify her job to the Regents. So many interviews completed, requiring so many person-hours, requiring an adjustment and increase in salaries and personnel for the counseling department; in these days of unemployment it was necessary to keep one's forms in order.

"But," Kevin stammered. He almost lost control of his voice, but regained it with effort, and continued to keep a respectful tone. "I got A's in those

16

courses," Kevin said. "A's at Northridge, B's in the courses here. What difference does it make if I had the prerequisites if I got B's here? Prerequisites are supposed to keep you out of work you can't handle, but it's obvious that I *can* handle the work, because I *did*. Please, ma'am, can't you do something to help me?"

She held her head high and her look of sympathy was patently artificial. "We have to go by the rules," Ms. Rasmussen said. "There was a mistake. You should never have been admitted to the courses here without proper prerequisites. Now, officially, you have never taken those courses at all. You'll have to go meet the prerequisite requirements, then take the courses over again. I'm very sorry." She wasn't.

"But that's two years of my life!" Kevin said. He wasn't deferential now. "You can't do that to me!"

Patiently Ms. Rasmussen punched in more numbers. A blur of fine print filled the screen. "Look," she said. "Here are the rules. You may read them for yourself—"

If I plead, Kevin thought. If I plead, I may, just may, get her to help. She wants to feel important, and I can help her. Just say the right words.

But the feeling of self-contempt was too strong. His control broke like an exploded dam. "Damn you to hell!" he shouted.

"You will not swear at me." Ms. Rasmussen stood. "Get out of here. Instantly. I will not have students shouting at me. I do not have to put up with that. If you don't leave I will call the Campus Police."

Police. He didn't want trouble with the police. Kevin stood. "I'm very sorry," he said "I should not have lost my temper—"

"Go." Now that she was in control, Ms. Rasmussen felt much better. "Go now."

"Yes," Kevin said. He turned.

"Wait." The counselor kept him standing for a long moment. Her smile, a thin wintry smile that showed the tiniest thin line of white teeth, played at her lips. "You forgot your ID card. That's very important, you will need it. Here." She laid it on the desk, although it would have been easier to hand it to him.

Kevin took the card and left. As he went out, Ms. Rasmussen was marking the time onto still another form. The form title was "Interviews Successfully Completed."

*   *   *

He walked home glumly, not knowing what to do. There was a Zero-Growth Movement rally on campus, and students were shouting. An alternate technology group was arguing with the Z-G's, screaming that all technology wasn't bad, only the big industries. Another group of Social Technocrats appeared to argue for high technology owned by the people. The Campus Police stood by interestedly.

He walked in fury, not knowing whether to be angry with himself for losing his temper when he might have talked Ms. Rasmussen into doing something for him, or for not telling her exactly what he thought of her and her useless bureaucratic job; whether to be ashamed for not getting the results he wanted, or for trying when trying meant pretending respect for the Rasmussens of this world.

When he reached the top of the stairs he wasn't surprised to see the door to his room standing open. Mrs. Jeffries often brought food to the students' rooms and put it in their 'frigs. She said she cooked too much, but she did it often. Kevin went in without thinking.

The room was empty. All his books had been tumbled from the shelves onto the floor. His calculator was a heap of rubble in the center of the floor. The refrigerator door stood open, and everything that had been in it was poured into a hideous soup over his books.

When he went into the bathroom he found Snowdrop drowned in the toilet.

III

"Dr. Farrington?"

"Yes, Kevin?"

"Can I see you for a moment, sir? I need help."

"Sure." Professor Farrington's grin was reassuring. Of all Kevin's professors, Farrington was the only one who seemed actually interested in the students. He was a bulky man, heavyset and going to fat; forty years before he'd been a football star, but he had little time for physical activities now.

His classes were interesting. He taught what was in the books but he often spoke of other things as well, of a world remade by technology and engineering, of man's future. "We're in a bad phase right now," Farrington said many times, "but that won't last. These things come in waves. Right now the social theorists are on top, and they don't trust people. It won't last. You'll all live to see a new era, an era of freedom and individual responsibilities, and I want you to be ready for it."

He waved Kevin toward his office and followed along the hall. His steps were slow; Farrington seemed always physically tired, but he spoke with an animation that denied it. They went into the office, a large room lined with books, drafting table beneath the windows, a large read-out screen on the battered wood desk. "Have a seat," Farrington said. "Now, what can I do for you?"

Kevin showed him the computer letter and described his interview with Ms. Rasmussen. "And I can't afford two more years," he concluded. "It's just not fair."

"No, probably not. Fair play isn't the strongest point of our regulated welfare state. Rules and order, that's our goal. Let me have your ID card, I need to look up your records."

Kevin handed it over. "Two years because a computer says so. That doesn't make sense."

"Makes more than you think." Farrington inserted the ID card into a slot in the desk console. He began punching in numbers. "When you admit everyone who wants to go to college, and you're not allowed to flunk anybody out, you have to have some way to keep from getting hip-deep in idiots-with-degrees," Farrington said "Too bad it happened to the engineering school too. I remember when this kind of horse puckey was reserved for the Sociology and Education Departments. And law schools, of course."

"But can't you do something?"

Farrington studied the read-outs. "Probably not. Used to be the professors had some authority here, but not for a long time now. Rules are rules—"

"Not you too!"

"Easy. Doesn't do any good to get excited. Least not here, not with me. Kevin, I can understand why you young people get frustrated. If things like this had happened to me when I was your age I'd have been scheming on how to bring the whole mess down in blood. I don't suppose your generation even talks like that."

Kevin said nothing. Farrington was right. A couple of times Kevin had complained about some rule or another, tried to get a student protest together, and his classmates had thought he was crazy. The only student demonstrations to get involved in were those sponsored by one of the recognized outfits. Demonstrating for the right causes was a key to a good job after graduation. Making trouble was a way to welfare.

"I can't give you a degree by waving my hand," Farrington said. "But we can diddle the system a bit. You stay on. I'll see that you get admitted to graduate courses. You can enroll in these junk courses they want you to take again, but you won't have to go to class. Just show up on exam day. When you've touched all the bases you'll get your degree and have two years of advanced study to go with it. Get you a better job."

"It sounds good," Kevin said, "But I can't do it—"

"I wasn't through," Farrington said. "Look, I've got some buddies out at Systems Development Corporation. I can get you on part-time as a draftsman at SDC. Get you some experience programming, feeding problems into the computer, that sort of thing. Won't pay too bad, and you'll have job experience in your resume. Ought to about make up for the time this stupid system is costing you."

22

"But I still can't," Kevin said. "I'd love to. What you're offering is better than —Dr. Farrington, it would be great, and I really thank you, but I can't stay in Los Angeles."

Farrington frowned. "Why not?"

Kevin told him. "I might have thought it wasn't serious, but when I found Snowdrop in the toilet—" He couldn't finish. The memory of wet fur was in his nostrils.

Farrington's lips tightened. "You know, a few years ago—I guess it was longer than that. Back about 1980. I knew a guy named Turk. Sold custom car parts. One of those damned street gangs decided Turk ought to kick in to them. Pay protection.

"The cops couldn't do anything: judges didn't believe in juvenile criminals. 'No such thing as a bad child,' all that crap. One day Turk came home and found his dog puking blood all over the carpet. Seems someone had fed it meat filled with ground glass. So Turk went hunting. He took a shotgun over to the gang headquarters and blew hell out of the place. Then he cruised around the city looking for their cars and blew off four or five. You know, old Turk lived another two, three years, finally died of a very natural heart attack. I understand that gang still goes out to the cemetery every month to be sure Turk's still under ground."

"I couldn't do that!" There was horror in Kevin's voice.

"No, I don't reckon you could. Mind if I look up your psych records?"

"No, sir."

Farrington played with the console keys. A series of graphs came onto the screen. "Know what these mean?"

"No. They wouldn't let me take any advanced psych courses. I don't know why."

"I do," Farrington said. He pointed to a series of dips and valleys on one of the graphs. "Those little wiggles right there. Unstable. Potential for violence. You got a hot temper?"

"Sometimes. I try to control it," Kevin said.

"Yeah. You've got some other problems too. Kind of a misfit, aren't you?"

"No!" Kevin almost shouted it. "I get along!"

"Have many friends?"

"Yes—well, I don't have time to make many friends. But I get along."

"Sure," Farrington said. "But I expect you have to work on that individualist streak. I see they had you in for intensive counseling for a couple of years. Help any?"

"Sure. Sensitivity training is important, particularly for those who hope to be promoted into managerial positions—"

"You don't need to quote the goddam course prospectus to me." Farrington said. He leaned back in his big chair. "Kevin, when I was your age, an engineer built things. Took responsibilities. They'd give us a project and by God we'd get it done. Build a bridge. Design something. Start with paper and ideas and see it through until it worked. Nowadays they put you in a room full of people just like yourself, and you feed numbers into a computer. Somebody checks all your work, somebody else originated it, and a third type will supervise the hardware—do you think you'll like that?"

"No," Kevin admitted. "But what can I do?"

Farrington shrugged. "Not much. Not here, anyway."

"I mean," Kevin said, "the system's so set up that no one person can ruin things for everybody. Isn't that the way it's supposed to work?"

"Sure. How it's supposed to work." Farrington fingered the computer letter that lay on his desk, then looked back at the console. He seemed to be debating with himself. "Senecal, I'm going to tell you something that I don't want you to repeat. You say I told you this, and I'll deny it."

"Sir? I can—I don't have to tell people everything I know."

"No. I don't expect you do," Farrington said. "Look, that computer letter was no accident. The psych people have decided you're not ready to graduate. If they hadn't found problems with your prerequisites they'd have come up with something else."

"But—why?"

"You're not mature enough. Not group-adjusted. See those little code numbers? That's the clue."

Kevin leaned over the desk and looked at the read-out screen. The numbers meant nothing to him. "I don't think those were on the printouts I got," Kevin said. "I sent for my records. Don't they have to tell us everything in them? I thought there was a law—"

"Oh, there are laws and laws," Farrington said.

"One law says that if properly qualified human-resources specialists determine that giving a subject information would be damaging to the subject, the information can be withheld. There are some others, too. I'm not even supposed to be able to get this, not even with your ID card, but—well, a couple of my old students designed the computer security system. Anyway. The Psych boys have decided you ought to stay on as a student a couple more years. Then they'll decide if your new profile is good enough to let you have a degree. My guess is that it'll still be 'no,' and it won't matter if you stay on as an undergraduate until you're ninety."

"But what can I do?" Kevin demanded.

"I don't know. One of the unions might help you, but you can't join a good union without a degree. Got any pull? Political friends? Ever worked campaigns?"

"No."

"Then I can't think of anything. I wish I could help. I really do." Farrington opened his desk drawer and took out a printed brochure. "There's one thing. This outfit's looking for good general systems engineers, and they don't care about degrees. They want ability, and I think you've got signs of that. You did a good paper for me last term. I'll recommend you, if you like." He scaled the brochure across the desk.

The illustration on the front leaped out at him; space as black as night; the Milky Way a sparkling waterfall of stars. Against the backdrop hung a small rock. Men floated in the foreground. A large mirror focussed solar energy onto the asteroid, boiling out metals.

"The Daedalus Corporation," Kevin said. "That's a deep-space outfit."

Farrington nodded. "One of them. And they're hungry. Want me to talk to them for you?"

Kevin knew there were companies operating in the Asteroid Belt, but he'd never thought of working for one of them. When he thought of going to space it was always in terms of one of the near-Earth orbiting factories, or possibly to the Hansen-MacKenzie base on the Moon. There was real money to be made in the industrial satellite factories—and you could come home to spend it.

"Nobody ever comes back from the Belt," Kevin said.

"Not many have, yet," Farrington agreed. "But maybe they don't want to come home. They're doing something real out there in the Belt, Kevin. Something important for the whole human race, and it's not done with acres of engineers sitting in bullpens. They're going to build a whole new civilization out there—and maybe save this one in the bargain. If I were your age I wouldn't hesitate a minute."

For a moment the intensity of Farrington's tone, the professor's sincerity and wistful expression, made it sound attractive. Kevin thought again. He knew almost nothing about the Belt. There were stories. That they'd found fabulously rich sources of metals, millions of tons of nearly pure iron and nickel and copper, with solar energy to run the refineries. "But they've never brought anything back," Kevin said aloud.

"No. And if they don't pretty soon things will be bad for the asteroid industries," Farrington said.

"But that's just the point. They need people out there. People who'll work—"

"How can they bring enough metal back to Earth to matter? The asteroids are a long way out."

"There are ways," Farrington said.

"I just don't know—"

"Yes." Farrington sighed. "I know. You've been brought up to think somebody will take care of you. Social Security, National Health Plan, Federal Burial Insurance. Family Assistance, Food Stamps, Welfare. Union representatives to speak for you. And I'm talking about a place where it's all up to you, where you take care of yourself because nobody's going to do it for you. I guess that can be scary to modern kids. You don't like the idea, do you?"

"It's not that," Kevin said. "But I never really thought about the Belt. It's not what I had in mind for myself—I'm sorry."

"Nothing to be sorry about. It's an alien way of life. For you. Me, I wish I was young enough to go. Enough of that. Kevin, I'll think about your problem. Maybe we can come up with something. Now, if you'll excuse me, I've got to prepare for my next class."

"Yes, sir. Thank you."

"Nothing to thank me for. I wish I could have been some help. Nice seeing you. Drop in again—I mean that. Come see me again in a couple of days. Maybe I'll have thought of something."

"Thank you. I will." But you probably won't have thought of anything, Kevin thought as he left the office.

Alfred Farrington continued to stare at the computer read-out screen. He took out a thin black notebook and copied some of the data into it, then frowned and selected a name on a roller index attached to the input console. He pushed a button and the phone dialed itself. It rang twice.

"Yeah?" The phone showed a fat man about Farrington's age.

"Alf. How are you, Ben?"

"Fine, except for recruiting—"

"Yes. I thought I had you a good prospect, but he may not work out. Then again, he may."

"Something special about this one?"

"Good prospect. No family ties, nobody's going to worry about him, nothing here for him to spend money on. Engineering student. And a pretty good one compared to the lot we get now."

"Umm. The ship's leaving pretty soon. Think you can get him aboard? We're short on engineering talent. I've been thinking maybe we ought to ask Paul to send out a couple of the Order—"

"Possibly. I hope it doesn't come to that. I doubt if he'd do it," Farrington said. "We've few enough in the Fellowship. Better to hire some talent—"

"If we can. One way or another we've got to get moving *now*, or the whole thing's going to come apart. How good is this prospect?"

"Potentially quite good. And no family. No one will worry about where he's gone or when he's coming back."

"Good."

"Of course his motivation's all wrong," Farrington said thoughtfully.

"To hell with motivation," Ben said. "Get him aboard. We'll motivate him. And if we can't, well, we can still get some use out of him."

"Yes. Well, I'll send you his records. If you like him, let me know. There may be more pressures I can put on him. Now what about those others I sent over?"

They talked for a long time.

* * *

The new locks to Kevin's room hadn't been disturbed. The door hadn't been opened. It hadn't had to be.

Kevin's black tomcat was nailed to the door. The cat mewed piteously. Kevin gulped hard and examined the wounds. He knew what had to be done, and after a moment he did it. Then he sat on the floor with tears streaming from his eyes.

After a while he heard steps behind him. Sergeant Mason came into the upstairs hallway.

"Your landlady called," the policeman said. "The desk man passed it on to me." He looked at the still body nailed to the door. "You got your keys?"

"Yes—"

"Go inside. Carefully. Here, let me open that. You get back over there." Mason used the keys, stood back and kicked the door open. The room hadn't been disturbed. "I'd say it's all right." Mason said. "They don't usually do anything final after a warning like—like that. Not for a couple of days. Go get your face cleaned up, son. Go on, get."

Kevin went to the washroom. When he came

back the body was gone. Sergeant Mason was sponging off the dark spots on the door.

"That's not evidence either, I suppose," Kevin said. His voice held bitterness.

"Evidence? Sure it's evidence. Of childish pranks. Cruel, of course, but deprived children often express aggression in cruelty. It's relatively harmless. We must weigh the importance of human life against that of an animal, and of course there can be only one decision—look, kid, I'm not saying what I believe, I'm just quoting."

"Children! They're no better than animals! Bad animals."

"Sure. You know that. I know it. But make the DA and the judges believe it—Look, son, the judges are picked by the lawyers, and the lawyers get paid by the government to defend these deprived kids. The lawyers all live in closed communities with rent-a-cops. So do the newscritters. Nobody kills *their* pets. It's the way things are. You just get your degree and get out of LA, go find a good job and live in a company town with company cops around, and you can forget all this—"

The policeman's face went hard. "Look, I don't like it either. I can give you some protection, but we've only got so many police. And the Green Fence is never going to forget that you killed one of theirs. They'll remember a long time. A *long* time, Kevin."

"But this is insane!" Kevin sat on the couch and looked at the familiar books—stained and damaged now— on all the walls. The world no longer made any sense. "You're telling me this gang is more powerful than the government!"

Mason shrugged. "Maybe. What do you want us to do? Go lean on those kids? Rig up evidence? Senecal, I've got nineteen years in. I can retire in another year. You got any idea what happens to cops who bend the rules that way? The Public Defender and the Civil Liberties Union and all the others would have my head on a platter! Sure, there's lots of us would like to get those scumbags off the streets any way we can. But we've learned better, Senecal. They got Lieutenant Mogowa for tampering with evidence and they sent him to prison. He lived about a week. Not me, son. Not me. I got a wife and three kids—and none of 'em cops either."

"So you'll wait until they kill me—"

"And then maybe I can nail 'em for it. And if I do they'll be on the streets in a year. Yeah. That's the way it is, Senecal. Got any more beer?"

"Yes, but you'll have to excuse me. I've got to go make a telephone call. Maybe I can catch Dr. Farrington in his office."

IV

Kevin had never seen so many forms and tests. There were dozens of them, and they asked him for information that no sane person would know. Finally he threw down his pencil. "This is ridiculous!" he shouted.

Three other job applicants who were still working looked up in annoyance, then went back to their tests. The test monitor, a pretty girl in short skirts, frowned. "You must complete your tests—"

"I will be damned if I will," Kevin said. He stalked out of the room as the girl pleaded with him to go back and finish.

That blows that, Kevin thought. Damnation. I thought a deep-space-operations outfit would—

"Congratulations, Senecal. Come with me, please." An elderly fat man barred his path. "Come on, we're running low on time," the man said. His voice was filled with authority.

Kevin wanted to tell him to stuff it, but he had nothing to lose. He followed the man through twisting hallways, then into an elevator. The man didn't speak until they got off at the top floor of the Santa Monica office building.

Downstairs the building had been coldly professional: new, expensive, and utterly without warmth. Up here it was completely different. The carpets were old but comfortable. Holos of space mining operations hung along the walls. People were dressed casually, and worked in small groups, or alone, and some sat in their offices with their feet on the desk and eyes directed to the ceiling. One man was making a paper airplane.

They went to the end of the hall and into an office. It too was comfortably furnished, and reminded Kevin of Professor Farrington's room.

"I'm Ben Simington," the fat man said. "Have a seat."

The chairs were comfortable.

"Want a drink? Scotch. Yes. I recommend scotch whiskey, a double."

Simington went to a wall panel, touched it, and let it swing open. An elaborate wet bar was behind it. He took out glasses carved with strange creatures and poured, then handed one to Kevin. The figure on Kevin's glass was a phoenix. "Cheers," Simington said.

Kevin lifted the glass and sipped. The whiskey was smooth, much better than any scotch he'd ever had before.

"Confused?" Simington asked.

"Yes."

"Think about it."

Kevin did. What data had he? The contrast between the lower floor of the Daedalus building, coldly professional, like hundreds of others all over the city, and the relaxed attitudes of the people on this floor—all of them obviously high-ranking executives even if they didn't act like it—was indeed confusing. This office, plain, but with very expensive carpets and pictures and electronic equipment—Kevin realized that he had, in all his life put together, never spent as much money as this office must have cost, yet the impression was of comfort and utility, not ostentation.

Then there were the tests. Medical exams, of course, then the others. The first ones had been sensible, related to systems engineering, digging deep into his knowledge. Others were obviously psychological tests, and all big companies used those. But after that—those forms, which asked for things like grandmother's age at death, great-grandfather's occupation, every address at which he ever lived. They'd made no sense, and they got worse as he went along. Why? What would the Daedalus Corporation want with such information?

Nothing. They couldn't want it. So why ask for it?

"You expected me to give up on those tests," Kevin said.

"Let's say we hoped you would. But not too soon. Part of the test score is the time it takes for the applicants to tell us to go to hell. Quit too soon, we don't need you. Not enough motivation. Keep on after it's too obvious the things are useless, and —well, you came off pretty good."

"But—"

"Many of the chaps down there still wading through will get jobs," the fat man said. "We need paper shufflers too. But we wouldn't send them out

35

to the Belt. I take it you do still want the job."

"Yes." Kevin's voice was unnecessarily strong. He realized that, but didn't explain.

"Why?" Ben Simington prompted.

"Because there's got to be something better than —" He didn't know how to finish. Better than here, where teenaged gangsters tortured cats and threatened people and the courts protected them. Better than a world where there were regulations upon regulations, where every detail of your working life was supervised by Federal inspectors and union officials, where you could get into trouble for working too hard, where they told you that all the regulation was the price of a stable world economy and then they couldn't protect you from street gangsters. Better than— "Better than always having forms to fill out and people who think the forms are important," he said.

Simington nodded. "Good. We need people who want their work to make sense. But don't get the idea that it always will, Kevin. Sometimes there's things to be done whether they make sense or not. Still, you won't find too much monkey motion out where you'll be going. You'll have to take care of yourself, but you won't mind that. Wish I could go along. Drink up."

Kevin took another healthy sip of excellent whiskey. It went down smoothly and warmed him from the inside out—that and the fat man's camaraderie. He liked the feeling. Kevin was intelligent enough to know it was all deliberate, that it was all planned to make him feel welcome, but he liked that too. These people wanted him, and they cared about how he felt.

They talked for an hour. The fat man looked at Kevin's test scores, his medical records, his file from UCLA—Kevin wondered how he'd gotten that, but didn't ask—and a lot of other subjects. Some didn't seem very important.

Finally Simington leaned back and looked pensively at the ceiling. "It's that time again," he said. "I have to make up my mind. Are you worth the investment?"

"I honestly don't know," Kevin said.

"Neither do I." The fat man sighed. "You'd think I'd have thousands of volunteers," he said. "And I do, but not qualified people. The Belt's not the same as a quick tour in orbit. Don't kid yourself that it is. They're spread thin out there. A couple of thousand people, mostly on Ceres, spread across billions of cubic miles. It's no picnic, Kevin."

"No." He hadn't expected a picnic. He thought about the vast emptiness of the Belt. It wasn't a place he'd go by choice—but what choices had he? There were *plenty* of volunteers for the factories orbiting Earth, and what use would Kevin Senecal be to one of them? Officially he was neither engineer nor good millhand. He was nothing. It wouldn't be that way in the Belt, and that was something to think about.

"*Wayfarer* leaves in four days," Simington said. "Can you be in her?"

"Four days! Mr. Simington, I don't really know anything about space industries, and I can't learn in four days!"

"We don't expect you to. Trip out takes nine months. You'll learn more about space operations than you really want to know. Nothing else to do aboard ship. There'll be a reader and plenty of tapes. Ship's crew drills you in equipment, p-suits, getting around outside. You'll learn to live in low gravity or you won't live at all. I'm not worried about what you'll know when you get to Ceres. It's whether you'll stick it out that bothers me."

"I generally finish what I start," Kevin said.

"Yep. One reason I'm talking to you is because your coach told me how you finished a game with two broken ribs. Didn't play too well, but you finished."

"That was in high school." Just how far back had Daedalus gone in checking his background? But it made sense: he was going to cost them a lot of money. "I still don't understand why you want me," Kevin said.

Simington shrugged. "Who do we send out, Kevin? Not superheroes trained for one mission; most of the astronauts came apart when their tour was over. Senior engineers? Why would they go? They're doing all right here. No, we've found our best people are misfits who don't like our modern welfare state. If they've got some other reason to get them headed for the Belt, that's fine; but it's what they do when they get there that counts." The fat man looked down at the data sheets on his desk. "Look, I don't believe in a lot of this psych garbage, but some of it's useful. In some ways I may know you better than you know yourself."

There wasn't anything Kevin could say to that.

"Contract's for five years," Simington said. "But we don't really make a lot of profit on five years. We need people who'll go the course." He went back to studying the read-outs.

Kevin suddenly wanted very badly to go. Partly it was a competitive urge. He didn't want to be told he wasn't good enough. But there was more, too. Out there he might find a meaningful job and a chance to do something important.

Earth was running out of metals, of oil, of coal, of everything. The anti-technology organizations had halted nuclear power development and Eco-freak rioters had smashed the space-power antenna outside Bakersfield—and investment money to build another couldn't be found. Population was rising and food production wasn't. There were already famines in parts of the world, and the pinch was felt everywhere, even in the United States. And the lawyers continued to gum up everything—in the courts, permit hearings, environmental impact statements.

The One Earth Society said the answer was to eliminate technology, space industries, everything that wasn't "natural." The costs would be terrible: millions, billions dead, but there was nothing else. Earth must abide, and she could not support a plague of mankind, an epidemic of humanity.

Kevin remembered Professor Farrington's lecture on that. "Maybe they're right," Farrington had said. "Maybe. But it's for damn sure if there's an alternative this is the time to take it. We can get off the Earth and live in the solar system. Not on one planet, but on nine of them, nine planets, thirty-five moons, and a million asteroids. Right now we can go. If we wait a few years, things will be so desperate down here we'll never make it. This is the first and last opportunity for mankind to be something more than a carnivorous ape crawling on the surface of one insignificant planet."

Kevin, remembering, nodded to himself. "I want to go," he said. "And I can make it in four days."

Simington said nothing for a long time. Kevin held his breath. Finally the fat man spoke. "Okay. I can offer you a starting salary of fourteen thousand Swiss francs a year. Five-year contract."

Kevin made rapid mental calculations. About a hundred and fifty thousand US dollars a year. It wasn't as high as he'd expected; not that high at all in these days of inflation and ultra-taxation. Engineers on Earth made more. Engineers in orbital factories made a *lot* more. But—it was more than he could get without degrees and a strong union.

"It's more than you think," Simington was saying. "We pay half that in francs in the Belt, the other half into your account in Zurich. We'll set that up for you. No point in letting Uncle Sugar get his hands on your money. If you don't have too much junk shipped out from Earth, you can save your return passage in about four years."

"And if I don't save?"

Simington shrugged. "Your problem. We pay your way out. If you stay ten years with us, we pay your way back in. Don't worry about it. Even if you can't cut it for us, you won't be out of a job. There's a lot more jobs than people in the Belt. You won't starve."

"I suppose not—"

"And we give you a sign-up bonus," Simington

said. "Thirty-five thousand bucks. You can use that to clean up any Earth-side problems. We'll also provide you with a basic outfit."

"Sounds good," Kevin said.

"It is good. We take care of our people. Notice I haven't said anything about owing us for passage and bounty. Some outfits pay higher, but their people owe for passage out. Some never do save it back. We don't work that way."

Sure, Kevin thought. But you're out to make a profit like the others.

Profit. Most of his professors had acted as if profits were nasty. Only Farrington seemed to think differently. And Wiley Ralston, of course. Not that the professors had any control; international firms survived despite the intellectuals' contempt. The welfare state could tax US corporations practically out of existence, but they couldn't get their hands on the internationals, or the space operations firms.

"What kind of work?" Kevin asked.

Simington's grin was wide. "Everything! Mining operations, living quarters, refinery design, ships and transport, agriculture—it all needs doing. Terrific opportunity."

If it's that great, why do you need me? Kevin wondered. But it sounded exciting, and besides, what other choice did he have? "I'll take it."

Simington nodded. "Report here, ready to leave, in two days."

* * *

They flew him down to the Baja California spaceport in a windowless transport. He crouched with his gear among empty cargo containers and tried not to think of what was coming next. There was only one other passenger, a man more than twice Kevin's age, shorter by five inches but weighing almost as much as Kevin did—built like a lineman rather than a half back. He had dark hair and brown eyes and a fine network of thin red lines around his mouth and across the bridge of his nose. He drank heavily from a hip flask.

"Drink?" he asked.

"No thanks."

The man shrugged. "Headed for *Wayfarer?*" When Kevin nodded the man's grin broadened. He put out his hand. "Me, too. Bill Dykes."

Kevin took the offered hand. Dykes's grip was firm. "Kevin Senecal." He waited for Dykes to comment on the name, but he didn't.

"Sure you don't want that drink? You look nervous."

"No, I'm not nervous," Kevin said. "Wish they had windows back here. I'd like to see Baja."

"Not much to see," Dykes said. "Railroads, power lines, highways, looks just like anyplace else now. Not like it was a few years ago when there wasn't but one road down here. Damndest thing. Of all the places in the world to put a spaceport, I'd have thought Baja would be the last."

The airplane engines thrummed on. Kevin was glad of someone to talk with. It took his mind off what was to come. Deep space, the Belt—but more terrifying was the way he'd get out there. "Good location," Kevin said. "Further south than Canaveral, so there's more eastward velocity. Takes less energy to get the pods in orbit. And it's on the ecliptic. Anything launched from there has an easier time of it getting to the Belt—" Kevin stopped, because he could see he was boring his companion. "Sorry. You know all this."

"Some," Dykes admitted.

"You've been up before?"

Dykes nodded. "Orbital factories. Three years in the General Motors satellite. Didn't want to join up for another hitch. Took my pay back to Earth."

"But—you must have saved a lot—"

"Sure, but the IRS got most of it." Dykes took another drink. "And I couldn't get a dirt-side job. My union's full of One Earthers. They say space technology takes jobs away from people on Earth. Sweet Lord, they fixed up an initiation fee that would've wiped me out! Tried working without a union, but you know how that is. Got beat up about as many times as I had a day's work."

Dykes didn't seem broken up about his problems. He smiled cheerfully and took another drink, a long one this time. "So I took what was left of my savings and headed for the Moon."

"Oh." The Moon might be a good place to work. "Hansen colony?" Kevin asked.

"Naw, couldn't get on there. If MacKenzie and Hansen had been hiring, I'd probably still be up. No mickey mouse crap with Hansen, they tell me. Just hard work. Naw, I tried a little prospecting, a little mining. Luna's no good. Regulations, bureaucrats, lawyers, taxes—hell, it's no different from Earth. No chance to get anywhere."

"So you're going to the Belt?"

"Sure. So're you. What in hell are you so nervous about?"

Kevin laughed. "Didn't know it showed *that* much. I—have you been up in a laser pod before?"

"Yeah. Four times. Lived through all but the second one."

"Huh?"

"That one killed me." Dykes held his serious expression for a moment, then grinned. "Look, there's nothing to worry about."

"Sure," Kevin said. "Sure. Say, if you don't mind, I'll have a drink after all."

* * *

The plane set down in morning tropical heat. There was no wind. The airfield was located near the launching facility, but a large concrete terminal building blocked their view of the laser field beyond. They watched their baggage loaded onto a cart, then went into the terminal

There were few formalities. Kevin showed his ticket and was checked off a list. "First time up?" the clerk asked. When Kevin admitted it, he was sent down a long stairway.

"See you," Dykes called.

The passage led to a waiting room. There were a dozen other people there, mostly men older than he was, but a few women, and one family with two children. There was also a remarkably pretty girl. Kevin tentatively smiled at her, but she didn't respond, so he took out a book and began reading.

Presently a man in white coveralls came in and waited for their attention. He didn't say anything, just stood there until they were all looking at him.

He looked at the two children and shuddered.

"Anybody here can't follow instructions? I mean follow 'em to the letter?" he asked. "If so, speak up and save the Company some money. Save your lives, for that matter. You can get killed doing something stupid."

There was still no response. He shrugged. "I'm Hal Winstein, and I'm supposed to tell you groundhogs how to get from here to the orbit station alive. After that you're somebody else's worry.

"You all have pressure suits and helmets that fit? You should have turned them in for inspection. Everybody do that?"

There were murmurs, but no one said anything.

"Okay. Next. Anybody seriously suffer from claustrophobia? Course not, you wouldn't be here, but I'm supposed to ask. Now here's the drill. You'll go get your suits on and get checked out. Check-out includes vacuum test to be *sure* your equipment works. When the techs are happy with your gear, you'll go to the loading area and climb into a capsule.

"The capsules hold two hundred kilos each. That's approximately two people and their gear. We strap you in the webbing and you'll be there a while. Eventually the capsules move to the launch area, you'll hear a warning, and off you'll go at three gravities.

"Three gees isn't all that much if you're lying flat in the webbing. It goes on for a lot longer than you think it will, so don't get worried. When it stops you'll be in orbit. No weight."

"Free fall," Kevin muttered. He wondered how

he'd feel. People often got sick in space.

"That's the only tricky part," Winstein said. "You'll feel like you're falling forever. Don't panic and don't unstrap. Capsules with kids aboard will be taken into the orbiter airlock and opened there. The rest of you'll have to get to the orbiter through vacuum. There's only two important things to remember: do exactly what the crewman who comes for you says you should do, and never get completely unfastened. You'll have two safety lines. Be sure one is attached to something before you unclip the other. The crew will get you into the airlock if you cooperate. If you don't, you could get very dead. Understood?"

"I think I will walk," the family man said. The others didn't laugh.

"Don't want to scare you," Winstein said. "But you do want to take this serious. Any questions?"

There weren't many. Everyone there was a potential colonist or would work in one of the satellite factories. Laser launching was a lot cheaper than tickets on the shuttle, but the Hansen Company didn't particularly encourage passenger traffic on the laser system: they made bigger profits on freight. Finally Kevin raised his hand.

"Yeah?" Winstein said.

"Can we watch the launches? I've never seen one."

Winstein looked at his watch. "If you get through suit check fast, you can watch cargo go up for a few minutes. Then you'll have to get below and load on. Okay, through this door to the changing rooms. Find your own gear and get it on."

"What do we do with our clothes?" one man asked.

Winstein shrugged. "Carry 'em along if you don't go over the mass marked on your ticket. Or ship 'em to somebody. Or leave 'em here and we'll give 'em to local charities. Suit yourself. By the way —I don't advise anybody to fudge on total weight. You wouldn't really want us to think you mass less than you do. And we can't afford to lose the capsules."

V

There was very little privacy in the changing room. Only a screen separated men from women. The only facilities were a long bench and table on either side of the screen.

Kevin collected his pressure suit from the Hansen Company inspector who'd checked it out. "Nice gear," the technician said as he handed it over. "David Clarke makes the best, in my book."

One more datum to file away, Kevin thought. Daedalus Corporation didn't stint on equipment. They'd given him the best. He had his suit, and helmet, with radios and tool belts; a programmable pocket computer, the latest model he knew of, complete with a plug-in memory-reference unit that contained, along with much other data, just about every formula and table in the big Chemical Rubber Handbook; a lightweight Fiberglas suitcase, really more like a pressure-tight portable footlocker. It was all first class and it made him feel that he was important to the company.

The pressure suit went on like a diver's wet suit, and looked like one only not so thick. It fit very closely; he had to use talcum powder to get into it. Gloves dogged onto the ends of the sleeves, and a seal set firmly around his neck. He slipped into the boots, hung the small equipment bag over his shoulder, and reported back to the technicians.

They pulled and pinched, looking for loose spots. They didn't find any in Kevin's, but the next to come up was the girl he'd seen before, and after a moment they handed her a lump of what looked like clay. "Shove that under your breasts," the techncian said. "Yeah, right there. Don't leave any gaps."

"But—" She was obviously embarrassed.

"Lady, you're going into vacuum," the man explained. "Your innards will be pressured to about seven pounds by the air in your helmet. Outside is nothing. Your skin won't hold that. The suit will, but you've got to be flat against the suit, otherwise *you'll* swell up to fill any empty spaces. It won't do a lot of good for your figure."

"Oh. Thank you," she said. She turned away and used the clay as she'd been told.

The technician looked at Kevin and shook his head. "Don't get many small-town chicks here. Okay, sport, on with your helmet. See it's dogged right. Don't like to lose passengers in the test chamber."

The helmet fit snugly onto the neck seal. The technician checked the locking mechanism and seemed satisfied. "Okay, you and blondie there, into the next room and through the airlock." He raised his voice. "Sending in the first two, Charlie."

"Right. Come on, come on, we got a full schedule today."

Kevin and the girl went through the door and were motioned to another, this one steel with a large locking wheel. Through that was a large chamber. There was a man in a pressure suit inside it. He motioned to hoses on the bulkhead. "Connect up to those."

They did, and the man checked the fittings. "Okay," he said. "We'll pump out this chamber. As we do, there'll come pressure into your helmets through those hoses. When the outside pressure's gone, you're going to be uncomfortable for a while. Any gas in your system will expand until you'll feel like a balloon. Don't be too damned polite to get rid of it, or you'll be sorry. If you feel really uncomfortable, or your ears hurt real bad, or you can't breathe, hit one of those panic buttons next to you there. Otherwise, don't do anything at all. Understood?"

"Yes," the girl said. Kevin nodded.

"Right." Charlie turned to his control panel and pressed buttons. The outside door had already been closed and sealed while he was talking.

Kevin felt the pressure drop. His ears clogged for a moment and he swallowed frantically until they popped and were clear. The pressure continued to fall and he felt his insides swelling as Charlie had said they would.

"OKAY." Charlie's voice was loud in his headset. "I've got your pressures here. Everything looks right to me. Any problems?"

"No," the girl's voice said.

"Good. Now comes the hard part. The worst thing that can happen to you is to run low on oxygen. You won't know it's happening. So, I'm gonna cut down on your oxygen supply to let you get used to what anoxia feels like. While I'm doing it I want you to write your name on that pad there in front of you. Every time I say 'write,' you write your name until I say to stop. Okay?"

"Yes," the girl's voice said in his headset.

"Sure," Kevin said.

"You, mister, I asked if it was understood," Charlie said.

"Oh." Kevin turned on his microphone. "Sorry. Understood."

"Okay. Here we go. Write."

It was no problem. He wrote carefully, then glanced over at the girl. 'Ellen MacMillan.' Her handwriting was neat and precise, unlike his own heavy scrawl.

"Write," Charlie said, and they did it again.

It seemed a silly game. Kevin felt an urgent impulse to laugh. Why? part of his mind wondered. But it didn't matter, of course he wanted to laugh, this was silly—

"Write."

His hand didn't work properly, but it was all right, he was tired of this silly game. He glanced over at Ellen's paper. Her neat hand had written 'Coca-cola.'

'Scotch and soda,' Kevin wrote.

"Write."

'Will you have dinner with me?' he tried to write, but it didn't come out that way. He couldn't read it. Oh, well. Ellen looked at him and giggled. He responded, and they laughed together.

"Hey, you're beautiful," Kevin shouted.

She laughed harder. Why was she laughing? Kevin wondered. It was true enough. Well, maybe not beautiful. But she was nice, a really pretty girl, blonde curls cut off short but still long enough to curl. He stared at her pressure suit, trying to see where her breasts left off and the clay began. She saw what he was doing and patted the spot, giggling again.

"Write your names. It is very important that you write your names. If you do not write your names legibly you will not be permitted to go up today," Charlie said. His voice was very stern, and that was funny too.

Only, part of his mind said, it wasn't funny. He tried very hard, but all he could produce was a scrawl. Ought to be good enough, though, he thought. They can read that—

His head began to clear suddenly, and he looked at the paper in front of him. It was awful. He wanted to cry—

He felt the chamber pressure rising. It became very warm in the capsule.

"Okay," Charlie said. "When I give the signal, disconnect from the hoses and go out the far door. Take those papers with you, and don't forget what you've learned. Anoxia sneaks up on you. You think you're doing all right, even when you're acting like a stupid drunk. If you remember that, you can function longer. Not a lot longer, but a little longer anyway."

* * *

The next stop was another supply counter, where

he picked up his reflective coveralls and tool belt. When he put them on over his pressure suit, and slung the tool belt around his waist, Kevin felt like a spacer. He knew better. There was a lot to learn, and he wouldn't even begin learning it until he was aboard *Wayfarer*; but the tool kit and professional equipment was at least a start. He asked directions to the observation balcony and was shown a stairway.

The balcony was empty. It gave a view of the wide valley on the other side of the terminal building from the airfield. The upper parts of the valley sides were covered with the tall *cardones* cactus plants, giants twenty feet tall and more, looking like cartoons of the desert cactus. There were even vultures perched in the cactus. Below, on the valley floor, were the lasers.

At first it looked like a field of mirrors. Over a hundred lasers were scattered across the brown Baja desert sand. Each sent its output into a mirror. The mirrors were all arranged so that they reflected onto one very large mirror nearly a kilometer beyond the balcony.

A rail track ran onto a platform above the final mirror. Squat capsules, like enormously swollen artillery shells, sat on cars on the track, a long line of them waiting for launch. As he watched, one of the capsules was wheeled along the track until it stopped over the launching mirror.

The field became a blaze of blue-green light as the lasers went on. Somewhere nearby, Kevin knew, were two large nuclear power plants. They poured their entire output into the lasers below him, enough electricity to power a city, all turned into laser light. The mirrors pivoted slightly so that all their energy went to the one large mirror at the end of the field.

The capsule rose, suddenly and silently, as if pushed into the sky by a rapidly growing giant blue-green beanstalk. It vanished in seconds, but the laser beam continued to follow it, moving from vertical to an angle toward the east. Finally all the lasers went out together.

"My God," Kevin said aloud. "I'm going up like *that*?"

He heard a laugh behind him and turned quickly to see the girl who'd been in the altitude chamber with him. She smiled as he looked at her. "Yes, we are," she said. "Scared?"

"Damn betcha."

"Me too. I wish I'd taken the shuttle."

Another capsule was in position, and rose silently from the platform, vanishing into the clear blue sky, followed by the silent beam of intense light. If he listened carefully Kevin thought he could hear the hum of the beam. It was pulsed at something like two hundred times a second.

The laser system worked like a ram jet. Under each capsule was a bell-shaped chamber, open at the bottom. The laser energy entered the chamber and heated the air inside. The air rushed out, pushing the capsule upward. Then the beam was turned off just long enough for more air to get into the chamber, to be heated by the next pulse of the beam.

"I'm still not sure I believe it works," Kevin

said. "It looks like black magic."

"Green magic," Ellen said.

There was a long pause in the launching sequence, then a trainload of capsules came out. Each capsule was accompanied by an armed guard. Four Mexican Army tanks rolled alongside the train.

"Ye gods, that must be a valuable cargo," Kevin said. He looked quickly at Ellen when she didn't answer. She was watching them with a look of satisfaction. "Do you know what's in them?" Kevin asked.

"No, do you?"

"I thought you were watching as if you did. No, I haven't a clue."

"As you said, it must be valuable." She continued to stare until all the capsules were launched, and the guards and tanks rolled away. Then she looked at her watch. "Maybe we ought to be getting down—"

"Yes. Hate to miss the ship. Where are you headed?"

"*Wayfarer. Das Wanderer.*"

Kevin had thought she would be going up to one of the orbital factories. "All the way to Ceres? Alone?"

"Yes, why not?"

Kevin shrugged. "No reason."

"Except that you don't approve of women going to the Belt," she said. "That's man's work. I suppose you want restrictive laws for space, too. 'One job per family' out in the Belt as well as here on Earth." There was anger in her voice. "Well, you had that in the United States, still do really, but you won't get it in space, and I'm going whether you approve or not." She turned and stalked down the stairwell.

"Hey," Kevin called. "Hey, I didn't mean anything. I'm sorry—"

She didn't turn. To hell with her, Kevin thought. He slowed down, wondering what to do next.

"Kev! Hey, buddy," someone called.

Kevin turned. It was Wiley Ralston. "Wiley! Hey, are you going up this round?" Wiley had left Los Angeles two weeks before to find a job in deep space. Kevin wasn't that surprised to see him.

"Sure, I'm in the afternoon wave. Ride up with me?"

"Can't," Kevin said. "I'm going right now— hey, where are you going?"

"Got some things to arrange," Wiley said.

"You going in *Wayfarer*?"

"Right—you too?" Wiley was hurrying away, and his manner indicated that he didn't want to be followed. "You're going up right now? Not in the first capsule, though—"

"Sure, get it over with," Kevin said. He had to shout now; Wiley was moving away fast.

"Not the first," Wiley said. "Get on the last one—"

"Why?"

"Can't stop to talk, old chum. I've really got to scoot. See you aboard *Wayfarer*." He vanished into a door marked AUTHORIZED PERSONNEL ONLY, leaving Kevin standing in the middle of the empty corridor.

Damn, Kevin thought. He walked slowly to the capsule loading area. If I wait, he thought, I'll be scared out of my wits before it happens. He knew the laser launching system was safe, but that didn't stop the butterflies in his stomach.

May as well get it over with, he thought. He collected his helmet from the technicians.

There was one couple, and Ellen MacMillan, in the loading area.

"Who's first?" the technician asked.

"We are," the couple said.

"Right. Let's see you get into your hats and seal up." When they had their helmets dogged down the technician attached a pressure gauge to the man, looked worried, and said, "Go back and get a recheck on this."

"Something wrong?"

"Probably not, but I like to be careful. Okay, you're downchecked. Next." He jerked a thumb at Kevin, then at Ellen MacMillan. "You two. Get your heads on and let's hook up air bottles. Come on, we haven't got all day. Orbits don't wait."

When they had donned helmets and air tanks the technician checked his gauges again. "Looks good," he said, and sent them through a door. Kevin hurried along, trying not to think of the ride ahead. No worse than a roller coaster, he kept telling himself.

The launching pods were waiting. They seemed much larger than the ones he'd seen being launched, but even so the capsule was too small. It looked like a bell-shaped steel coffin. Ellen was already inside, strapping herself into a nylon-webbing couch. Kevin got in and lay on the other couch.

"Hear me all right?" a voice asked.

"Yes." They both answered at once, speaking a little too loudly, a little too confidently. Kevin turned toward Ellen to see that she was looking at him. They grinned faintly at each other.

"Fine. Now you wait a while," the tech's voice said. "Then you go. There's nothing tricky about any of this. You're hooked into the capsule air supply. When you make orbit you wait until a crewman comes and opens the can. Then—and not before—you pull that big lever above you. It disconnects you from the capsule system and you'll be on your own air tanks. You got two hours of air in the capsule and another hour in your tanks. Okay, I'm closin' you in. Bon voyage."

The capsule door closed. They watched the inside wheel turn as it was dogged shut. It already seemed close and cramped in the pod. Like a big steel coffin built for two, Kevin thought. He pushed the thought aside.

"We're moving," Ellen said.

There wasn't much sense of motion, but she was right. The capsule was moving along the track. Kevin tried to visualize its progress as it went inexorably toward the launch area. "Wonder how the kids will make out?"

"Better than us, I expect. At least we don't have to do anything—"

"I wish we did," Kevin said. "Better than just waiting for them."

"Sure—"

The warning tones sounded, then gravity seized them. They were pressed hard into the seat webbing.

Three gravities isn't all that bad; a little like being on a water bed with another mattress on top of you and two people piled onto that. It was possible to breathe, but not to talk. The acceleration went on and on.

I'm really going, Kevin thought. I've left Earth, and I won't be back for a long time.

* * *

Eventually the weight diminished, then was gone entirely. There was a sensation of falling, endless falling.

"I wonder if we made it," Ellen said. Her voice was artificially calm.

"Well, this is free fall—"

"Which we would feel whether or not we have enough velocity to make orbit," Ellen said. "And we won't know for about half an hour."

"By then the crew people will be here." I hope, Kevin thought.

There was nothing to do. There ought to be some kind of instrument to tell them they were in orbit. Kevin thought about that. How could you design one? No air, of course; couldn't measure velocity by air speed. An accelerometer hooked into the capsule; add up all the accelerations and you'd have velocity. A micro-computer to decide whether that was the proper velocity for the job. Sure, it could be done. Why hadn't they done it? Another expense for an already expensive business.

"I'd think someone would have spoken to us by now," Ellen said. She moved her arm up so that she could see her watch. "Only five minutes. Seems longer."

"Sure does. Uh—by the way, my name is Kevin."

"I know. I saw it on your paper. In the chamber. You read mine, too. We were pretty silly, weren't we?"

"Yeah. What outfit are you with?"

"None. I'm paying my own way," she said.

Good Lord. She had to be fabulously wealthy. He looked at her suit and other gear. First class, but no frills.

"How come you're taking the hard way up instead of the shuttle?"

"I couldn't afford a shuttle ticket."

That didn't make sense. "But you can afford a ticket to Ceres. Why are you going there?"

"It seemed like a good idea at the time," she said. Then she giggled. "I'm not too bad at engineering, Kevin, even if you don't approve of women in your business—"

"I never said—"

"And I didn't like the offers I got from the orbital factories. Or the Luna companies either. So I took what I could scrape up and bought a ticket. There wasn't much to spare."

"Out to make your fortune pioneering," Kevin said.

"That's right. There'll be good jobs for me. For anyone who can do the work. I see you don't approve."

"Sure I approve. It just seems like a long way to go—"

"You're going," she pointed out. "Why can't I?"

Kevin didn't answer. It just didn't seem right.

And you're a male chauvinist pig, he told himself. You hate to see a pretty girl working at something besides being a pretty girl.

Only that's not true. Dammit it's going to be rough out there, and—

And, he thought, I've got about three million years of evolution that says women and children shouldn't get into tough situations. The world is no longer a place where we live in caves and go hunt tigers, and our instincts are all fouled up, but we've got them.

Of course it was pretty rough for unmarried women in the United States anyway. The feminist movement had gotten legal equality for women— for a while. But then came the Equity scandals, and the Great Recession, and rising unemployment.

The unions put on the pressure, and Congress came up with the 'One Job Per Family' law. The courts threw it out, but Congress passed it again, and its status was still undecided. And women weren't welcome in most unions whatever the courts said, not with so many men out of work.

And maybe, Kevin thought, maybe the whole idea is wrong, but there are plenty of women— married women—who approve the job restrictions and reserved occupations.

"It seemed a long time from when they launched the cargo to when they sent us up," Kevin said. "How can both batches get to the same satellite?"

"They can't. The cargo went directly to *Wayfarer*. We go to the orbital station," Ellen said. She frowned. "I make it twenty minutes since we were launched. Doesn't that seem like an excessively long time? We ought to have heard from some-one."

"It does seem a while. Let's try calling out." He reached up to the radio panel above. There was a small card of instruction attached on its face. The first said, "FOR EMERGENCY USE ONLY" in five languages. "Is this an emergency?"

Ellen looked thoughtful. "I don't know—I'd hate to cause trouble, but I am getting a bit worried."

"Me too. To hell with them." He switched on the radio. Then he cursed. "There's no pilot light," he said. "Burned out—or does the set work?" There was only one way to find out. There was a jack on the face of the panel, and he plugged his mike into it. "Hey out there—anybody listening? This is Capsule—uh—nine-eight-four, hopefully in orbit. Anyone? Over."

"There isn't even static," Ellen said. "The receiver's not working. I doubt if the transmitter is working either."

Kevin looked at her with curiousity. She didn't seem scared. Or surprised, either. "What do we do?"

"You can try the transmitter again."

"Sure. Mayday. Mayday. This is Capsule nine-eight-four, Mayday, Mayday. Over." Again he heard nothing. How long would it take for one of the crewmen to get to them, if the transmitter worked but the receiver didn't? "Mayday, Mayday, Mayday. This is Capsule nine-eight-four. Our receiver is not working. We cannot hear your reply. Please come help us. Mayday."

Ellen began unfastening her seat straps. Kevin watched with a frown. They'd been told not to do that. Of course they'd also been told someone would come get them. He felt a knot of fear in his stomach. Trapped in an orbiting steel coffin. The sensation of falling was overwhelming now. In a moment he'd panic if he couldn't do something constructive. But what? "MAYDAY. MAYDAY. SOMEBODY COME HELP US!"

"I don't think that's going to do much good," Ellen said. She inspected the emergency set. "I don't see anything obviously wrong. Should we take the cover off and look?"

Kevin doubted that would be any use. Integrated circuit chips all look alike; how could you tell if something was wrong with one of them? He began unfastening his own straps. When they were loose, he floated away from the acceleration couch. It was a strange sensation. He'd seen people in free fall on TV often enough, and had looked forward to experiencing it, to being able to swim in the air, but now all he wanted was to get back to having weight again.

"We have suit radios," Ellen said. "Is yours powered?"

"Yes. Fresh batteries, and it was checked out yesterday—Hey! If we get outside this thing, we might be able to raise somebody with it."

"We'll have to disconnect from the capsule air supply before we can open the hatch," Ellen said. "If the hatch will open at all—"

"Why shouldn't it?"

She shrugged. The motion set her twisting slightly, and she caromed into him in the confined space. They both grabbed handholds.

"We have to do something," Kevin said. "Let's open the hatch." He reached for the big emergency disconnect handle.

"Wait. Fasten your safety line to something."

"Oh. Right." He clipped the line to one of the couch pipeframes. "Ready?"

"As I'll ever be. Go ahead."

He turned the red handle. It didn't turn; he did. Kevin cursed and got his feet planted against the couch, braced, and turned the handle again. It moved, slowly at first, then swung over. The ship's air hoses popped loose from their connections on their backpacks. They were now living on their air tanks.

"There's still pressure in here," Ellen said.

"Damn." She was right. The emergency disconnect was supposed to vent all the air from the capsule. The capsule hatch wouldn't open until the air was gone. There'd be no point in pulling on it; at seven pounds a square inch, hundreds of tons of air pressure held that hatch closed.

They couldn't open the hatch, and they had less than an hour of air.

VI

"I never thought they'd do it this way," Ellen said.

"Huh? Who'd do what this way?" Kevin asked.

"Nothing. We've got to bleed the pressure out of this capsule. Try to find the relief valve." She began searching her side of the capsule.

"This looks like it," Kevin said. There was a valve with a large handle. Remembering what happened the last time he'd tried to turn something in free fall, he braced himself before he twisted the handle.

It spun without effort. The handle wasn't splined to the valve stem. "Jesus Christ," he muttered. Ellen pulled herself over to watch as he futilely turned the handle. "No go," he announced. He was surprised at how calm he sounded.

"Your tool kit," Ellen said. "What's in it?"

Kevin didn't really know. He'd taken some of the items out to look them over, but that was something else he was supposed to learn about on the way out to the Belt, and there'd been so little time to prepare. He took the leather tool pack off his belt and opened it.

"There's a power head," he said. "I remember

that. And drill bits. But is it enough to get through the capsule walls?"

"You won't know until you try," Ellen said.

He took out the power head and inspected it. Then he searched through the loops of the tool pack until he found the drill chuck. It wasn't obvious how that attached to the power unit, but he worked carefully to be sure he didn't bend or break anything, and eventually it snapped into place. He pulled the trigger experimentally. The whine of the motor was delightful music.

"Now for the bit. About six millimeters? Looks about right." He squinted in the dim capsule light, trying to read the tiny words on the shank of the bit. He couldn't make them out. He hoped all the bits were intended for drilling metal. At least they were sharp and new.

He put the bit in the chuck and tightened it, then looked for a place to drill, choosing a spot between two braces. "I wonder how thick these things are."

"No thicker than they have to be," Ellen said.

"True." The less structural weight, the more payload. "Here goes." He pressed the bit against the metal surface and turned on the drill. It whirred reassuringly, and the bit threw up tiny bright chips that floated in the compartment, dancing about when stirred by air currents kicked up by Kevin's movements.

"It's working," Ellen said. For the first time there was excitement in her voice. "It really is."

He continued to drill, trying not to think about why he was drilling and where he was. That was no good, so he tried to think about something else.

Why was Ellen so calm? And why hadn't she been surprised?

The bit seemed to have gone awfully deep. Wouldn't it ever get through? But, even as he wondered, it jerked and pushed all the way to the chuck. Air whistled out past it. Kevin reversed the drill and withdrew it.

"Might take a long time to empty the capsule through that hole," Kevin said. "I'll do another hole, this time with a larger bit."

The second hole seemed to go easier. Now they could definitely feel the pressure dropping. He felt the familiar push of the neck seal as his air tanks pressurized his helmet in compensation. Then he glanced at his watch.

Fifteen minutes. They'd used a quarter of their air time in drilling the holes, and there was nothing they could do but wait.

* * *

"I have it," Ellen said. She turned the steel dogging wheel on the hatch. It seemed to turn easily, and the hatch opened inward.

Sunlight poured into the capsule. Kevin wondered how long that would last. They had to be in orbit, a very low orbit at that; it wouldn't be long before they were on Earth's night side. After making sure his safety line was still attached he slipped the pawl on the reel and worked his way out of the capsule. The sight was so glorious that for a moment he didn't move.

Earth was below, an enormous disc shrouded in wispy white clouds. They were above the Atlantic, and could see islands, and far at the horizon the west coast of Africa. It looked rather like an enormous circular map—they weren't high enough to see Earth as a sphere.

All around him—there was no "above" or "below"—there were capsules very close by. In the distance he saw what seemed to be a much larger structure that looked like a floating junk pile, without shape or form: a series of wheels and cylinders and shapes of no description at all held together by girders and cables. It had bright flashing lights. Kevin estimated it at about a mile away, although he found it was very hard to judge either its size or distance.

One of the channels of his suit radio was marked in red letters, for emergencies. Kevin turned to it, tongued the mike. "Mayday. Mayday, Mayday, this is Capsule—dammit!"

Ellen came beside him and put her helmet next to his. "Nine-eight-four."

"Mayday. This is Capsule nine-eight-four. Mayday! Dammit, where are you?"

"Maybe they aren't listening," Ellen said.

Her voice was the only thing he heard in his phones, and given that she was right next to him it didn't sound very loud at all; Kevin wondered if the batteries in his set were getting weak. But they couldn't be! They were new, the whole rig was new.

"Kevin, look! This is the only personnel capsule in this area. The others are all cargo."

She was right. There were plenty of capsules around, some only a few yards away, but the others were stubbier than theirs, and in contrast to the red-white checkerboard pattern on their own pod, these were yellow. Somehow they'd been launched into the cargo-pod recovery area. "Where are the others who came up with us?" Kevin demanded.

"Probably on the other side of the base station," Ellen said. "Where the crewmen are. No one will come over here until they have all the other passengers inside."

"But they damned well ought to know they're one pod and two people short," Kevin said angrily. "Now what? Mayday, dammit." They were conversing on the emergency channel. They shouldn't be doing that. Kevin laughed.

"What?"

"Hoping some communications monitor overhears us and comes out to slap us with a violation ticket." The joke seemed a little flat. He glanced at his watch. A little over half an hour of air. This was absurd! They were no more than a mile from the station—well, maybe two, Kevin thought; distances were hard to judge—and there wasn't any way they could get over there. Neither of them had a reaction pistol or a backpack jet. You can't swim in space: no air—nothing to push against! Kevin thought, sternly repressing an impulse to laugh hysterically. So what do we do? Have to do something!

"There are a lot of those capsules around here," Ellen said. "They seem to get pretty close to the station—"

Yes! Certainly they could get closer to the station. The nearest capsule in the right direction wasn't more than fifty meters off, possibly closer. It should be easy to jump that in free fall.

But if they missed, they'd drift forever.

He looked down at the reel on his safety line. Ninety meters. More than enough. "Look," he said. "I'm going to stay hooked on here and jump for that other capsule. If I hit, connect yourself to my line and I'll pull you over. Then we'll see about going on to the next one." He released the brake on his safety line reel.

She looked thoughtful for a moment, then nodded. "All right."

Kevin braced himself for the jump. No danger, not really. If he missed, she could pull him back. He crouched, got a hand-hold on the edge of the capsule hatch so he could get strain in his legs, and jumped.

He tumbled. Stars whirled above him, then Earth, the base station, Ellen, then more stars. He must have pushed harder with one leg than the other. He twisted to get a look at where he was going. The capsule he'd jumped for was a lot closer, moving up fast. He twisted again, instinctively spreading his arms and legs as wide as possible to slow his rotation.

His hand just brushed the capsule. He grabbed frantically and got hold of something. It almost yanked his arm off.

Have to remember that, he told himself: jump as hard as you can and you'll hit with the same force. "Okay, I'm aboard," he said. He clipped the other safety line to the protruding ring on the capsule. "Unsnap my other line and hang on—I'll pull you over."

"Right," she said. "Okay, I'm ready."

Kevin pulled gently. The temptation was to keep on pulling, but that wouldn't do: she'd just build up speed until she was moving too fast, maybe fast enough to get hurt. He let the line wind back onto its reel.

She turned just before she reached him and landed exactly feet first. She seemed pleased with herself. "Daddy made me study gymnastics," she said. "Always hated it, but now I'm glad I practiced."

"Yeah." Kevin pointed to another capsule, this one only twenty-five meters from their present position. "That one's a piece of cake. Here I go." He jumped, this time on center, and checked himself against his new perch.

It took time, but they were able to continue the process until they were only five hundred meters or so from the base. Then they ran out of capsules. Kevin prepared himself mentally for that final leap, one that he knew all too well would probably send him past the station, falling forever. . . . Better do it *now*—or he might not be able to do it at all. But wait—the station seemed enormous now; it had been farther away than he'd thought. He remembered that suit radios were deliberately under powered so they wouldn't carry too far; otherwise all of space would be filled with chatter. But the emergency frequency? And they were a lot closer than the last time he'd tried. "Hell, it's worth a try. Mayday. *Mayday,* dammit!"

"Hello Mayday, identify yourself."

"By God!" he shouted. "We made it. Hello. We were passengers aboard capsule nine-eight-four.

Air supply is going fast. We're on the leading side of the station, among the cargo capsules. Don't know which one. We abandoned the personnel pod and started hopping from cargo-pod to cargo-pod, trying to get to the base. I'd say we're about half a kilometer out."

"Nine-eight-four, can you make a light?" the voice asked. "I'll have a scooter out there in a moment. If you can show a light it will be easier to find you."

Kevin waved his flash. Down below he could see the sunset line stretching across East Africa. "Better hurry," he said. "We have about ten minutes of air left."

"No sweat. Be with you shortly."

* * *

"But how did it happen?" Kevin demanded.

The crewman shrugged. "I really don't know. There must have been a monumental foul-up down at ground control. Never happened before."

Foul-up at ground control. Sure, he thought. But why wasn't the capsule radio working? Or the emergency disconnect? Or even the manual pressure-bleed? It seemed like a lot of coincidences. It seemed like somebody was trying to kill him.

But that, he was sure, was silly. He couldn't think of anyone else who'd give a damn if he lived or died—and the Green Fence gang sure as hell couldn't reach out into space.

"I would appreciate it if you'd look into it," Ellen said. She seemed very calm. A lot calmer than Kevin was.

"Sure," the crewman said. "Luckily, no harm

done. We've just time to send someone out for your gear and get you aboard the scooter for *Wayfarer*. Come this way, please."

"But—"

"Kevin," Ellen said. "If we raise a fuss they'll have to investigate. We'll have to stay here. And *Wayfarer* won't wait. I didn't spend ten thousand francs for a ticket just to miss the ship."

"All right." He let the crewman lead him through the base. They were both being damned nonchalant about something that had almost killed them. Maybe this was the way it's done in space, he thought. It doesn't take much to kill you out here so nobody's impressed with close calls.

The crewman stayed to the outer rim. The station rotated to give artificial gravity, about forty percent of Earth's. Kevin was surprised to find that it was hard to tell just how much gravity he felt. After that time in no-weight, any gravity felt good.

The deck curved up in front and behind them, but it always felt level. It was a strange experience to be walking on a curve. The walls of the station seemed to be made of some kind of rubberized cloth with a metallic thread in it. They didn't feel hard to the touch, not like steel.

They went through several airlocks and came finally to one that led outside. The crewman unsnapped four new air bottles from a rack. Kevin started to put his two into his backpack.

"Suggestion," the crewman said.

"Yes?"

He pointed to an air gauge on the rack of bottles. "It's a good idea always to check and see if they're full." He reached into his own belt pouch and came up with a gauge. "Me, I don't even trust the airmaster's gauge. Use my own."

Kevin found one in his tool kit. Just for luck he checked one bottle with all three gauges, his own, the airmaster's and the crewman's. He got the same reading each time. Ellen followed his example.

"Now you're thinking. Okay, close up helmets and into the airlock."

* * *

The "scooter" was no more than an open framework with a long line of saddles and a rudimentary control system at its front. The passengers sat astride fuel tanks, and baggage was strapped underneath. The other passengers for *Wayfarer* were already aboard. Somebody waved at Kevin, and he recognized Bill Dykes. Ellen and Kevin got the last seats aft, the only two left. They strapped in, and about then a smaller scooter came up with the baggage from their capsule. It was lashed aboard, and the pilot hit the throttles.

The motion was very gentle, hardly any acceleration at all. The view was marvelous. There was Earth below, night with brilliant points and squares of city lights. Everywhere else were stars, countless stars, endless stars, an endless fall of stars in the Milky way, brilliant stars, with bright colors.

They moved through a clutter of space-launch capsules and crewmen with lights unloading them. Kevin looked at his watch. Ellen, behind him, noticed the gesture. By now they would have both been dead. She nodded at him then pointed to a channel on her radio. Kevin switched to it and turned on his set.

"I've never been up before," she said. "It's beautiful, isn't it?"

"Yes." They were coming to the daylight line on Earth below. It ran through the Pacific. Behind them were the bright spots that were cities crowded with their millions of people. Ahead and below was blue water, fleecy clouds and a distant line that might have been more clouds, or maybe California. To the north was a tight spiral of clouds.

"Typhoon," Ellen said. She stared frankly at it. She seemed on edge, but the way a tourist is excited at seeing new and wondrous sights, not afraid. If she can do it, so can I, Kevin thought. He was more shaken than he cared to admit.

Then there was more industrial activity around them. They were moving into full daylight, and Kevin was surprised to see how far they'd come from the base station in such a short time. Up ahead was a mirror larger than a football field. It just hung there in space. It focussed sunlight onto a rock somewhat larger than a house. Other big rocks nearby anchored what looked like big flat metal plates. Something—he supposed metal— boiled off the target rock and condensed onto the plates.

After that they saw a cage that looked as if it were made of ordinary chicken wire. It was a big, half a kilometer in diameter, and it was filled with launching pods, tanks of all sizes, rocks, spare scooters, what looked like big garbage cans, plastic bags—anything that wasn't in use at the moment. It kept things from drifting away.

They went past other marvels, and eventually *Wayfarer* came into sight. The scooter pilot pointed it out to them. "Your home for a while," he said.

Their first impression was of a bundle of huge cigars. Those were the big fuel tanks almost a hundred meters long. They were so large that they dwarfed the rest of the ship, and ran the entire length of midsection. Behind the "cigars" was a solid ring that held three rocket motors. Then at the end of a spine as long as the main body of the ship was the nuclear reactor and another rocket motor.

This was the real drive. The three chemical rockets were only for steering and close maneuvering. *Wayfarer's* power came from her atomic pile. The cigar-shaped tanks held hydrogen, which was pumped back to the reactor where it was heated up and spewed out through the rear nozzle. A ring of heavy shielding just forward of the reactor kept the pile's radiation from getting to the crew compartment. The rest of the pile wasn't shielded at all.

Despite the large size of the ship, the crew and cargo sections seemed quite small. There were some structures reaching back from the forward ring where the control room was. Two of those were passenger quarters. The other was another nuclear power unit to make electricity to run the environmental control equipment, furnish light for the plants, power to reprocess air, and all the other things the ship and passengers and crew would need. There was a big telescope and a number of radar antennae on the forward section.

The scooter pilot was careful not to get near the reactor in the ship's "stinger." He brought them in to the bow. The outer door of an airlock stood invitingly open. A crewman brought a cable over and attached it to the scooter, and then hauled the scooter in close. Then the passengers began the trip from their saddles into the airlock, crawling across the cable like so many spiders.

When it came his turn Kevin judged the distance and decided to jump. He had just crouched when the pilot grabbed him. "Hey, no!" the pilot shouted. "Not your first time in space!"

Kevin shrugged and grinned into his helmet. Probably he'd have to take extra-vehicular-activity training while on *Wayfarer*. As if he hadn't learned the hard way how to jump around in free fall . . .

He crawled across the cable behind the others.

Home at last, he thought. For nine months. A long time.

VII

The ship had been designed for sixty passengers. She carried twice that number plus eight crew. Most of the passengers were already aboard; *Wayfarer* was crowded. No more than half the passengers had ever been into space before, and everyone drifted through the ship in total confusion.

The internal space was constructed in a series of circular decks. Each deck had an eight-foot hole in its center, so that from the forward end, just aft of the separately enclosed control cabin, Kevin could look all the way aft to the stern bulkhead. Although there was a long and rather flimsy-appearing steel ladder stretching from aft to forward bulkhead, no one used it. Passengers and crew dived from deck to deck in the null-gravity conditions of orbit. Most of the passengers weren't very good at it yet.

A harried crewman in red coveralls punched Kevin's name into a console. "F-12," he said.

"If that's supposed to mean something, it doesn't," Kevin said.

"F deck," the crewman said "A deck is the bridge. B is the wardroom. C, D, and E are the three aft of that. E happens to be the recreation and environmental control. Yours is the one beyond that. They're marked." Someone else had come up and the crewman turned away. "You'll find it," he said over his shoulder.

Kevin shrugged. It was a mistake, because it caused him to drift away from his handhold. He grabbed frantically at a protruding handle—the ship had plenty of those—and when he was stable, launched himself down through the central well. He got past C and D decks before he had to catch something and try again. Since he was carrying his bulky Fiberglas travel case with all his luggage, he felt he had a right to be proud of his first efforts.

Finally he reached F deck, which he found to be sectioned into slice-of-pie compartments arranged in a ring around the central well, fifteen of them in all. He found the one marked "12" and went in.

His "stateroom" was partitioned off with a flexible, bright blue material that Kevin thought was probably nylon. The door was of the same stuff and tied off with strings. It didn't provide much privacy.

Inside the cramped quarters were facilities for two people. There were no bunks, but two blanket rolls strapped against the bulkhead indicated the sleeping arrangements. It made sense, Kevin thought. You didn't need soft mattresses in space. "Sleeping on a cloud" was literally true here. You needed straps to keep you from drifting away, but that was all.

One viewscreen with control console, a small worktable, and two lockers about the size of large briefcases completed the furnishings. The cabin wasn't an encouraging sight. Kevin wondered what he should do with his gear. His Fiberglas travel case was stuffed with things he'd been told he'd probably need for the trip; another larger case had been stowed somewhere by the crew and was inaccessible. He wandered out into the central area of F deck, and found that in other staterooms people were lashing their travel cases to the bulkheads. Kevin went back and did the same.

He wondered who his cabinmate would be. No one had asked him if he had any preferences. The only person he knew aboard *Wayfarer* was Ellen, and she wasn't likely to accept an offer to share quarters. While he was trying to convince himself that it couldn't hurt to ask, a middle-aged bearded man, quite heavyset, came in carrying two large travel cases. He looked up at Kevin apologetically.

"They told me to bunk here," he said. He blinked rapidly and looked around the small room. "It isn't very large, is it? I'm Jacob Norsedal." His voice wasn't very deep to begin with, and the low air pressure in the ship made it sound squeaky.

Kevin introduced himself. He tried to shake hands with Norsedal, but again got separated from his handhold and drifted across the cabin. Norsedal looked thoughtful, then, holding a wire conduit that ran through their stateroom, reached out and very gently pushed against Kevin. Kevin drifted to the bulkhead where he got himself back into control. Norsedal looked pleased.

The incident reminded Kevin that he was in free fall, and his stomach didn't like it much. He gulped hard. "I'll be glad when we're under way," he said.

"It won't last long, but it will be nice to have *some* weight again. Even for a day or so."

Norsedal frowned and rolled his eyes upward for a moment. "Not that long, I'm afraid," he said. "Let's see, total velocity change of about five kilometers a second, at a tenth of gravity acceleration — five thousand seconds." He took a pocket computer off his belt and punched numbers. "An hour and a half. Then we're back in zero-gravity." He restored the computer to its pouch. It was secured to it with a short elastic thong, as was everything else Norsedal carried.

Kevin was fascinated with the man. He went about everything methodically. First he strapped down his travel cases. Then he opened one. A geyser of clothing, papers, pencils, another and far more elaborate computer than the one he wore on his belt, chewing gum, bulbs of soft drinks, more clothing, a dozen magnetic-strip programs for his computer, and other small objects floated up into the room. They dispersed in the compartment.

"Oh, my," Norsedal said. He looked thoughtful. His hand snared the computer as it drifted by. Then he reached into the travel case again and got a shirt. "If you'll help me with this—"

Together they used the shirt like a seine to net all the gear. Norsedal produced a laundry bag to hold everything. Then he fished around in the travel case, more carefully this time, until he had a pleased expression. He came up with a small nylon-covered package that contained several rolls of Velcro, a pair of scissors, and a squeeze-tube of quick-drying glue. He began gluing Velcro hooks into his travel case and his locker. "I should have done this back on 'Earth," he said. His voice was almost perpetually apologetic. "But it wasn't certain I'd be coming, and they didn't give me the cases until just before I left."

Kevin watched interestedly. When the lockers were entirely lined with glued-on Velcro hooks, Norsedal carefully began work with the fuzzy Velcro, attaching strips to all his personal gear. Calculator, pencil case, notebook, tape recorder—

"That's a great idea," Kevin said.

"Want some? I brought plenty."

"Thanks, yes." Mostly Kevin was interested in the other man. He didn't seem like anyone Kevin would have thought would go to space. Norsedal was clearly overweight, very visibly so. He sniffed as if suffering from a sinus condition, and one of the objects Kevin had caught for him was a kit containing a hypodermic needle and bottles of what must have been room-temperature insulin. Although it was obvious that Norsedal had thought a lot about life in zero-gravity conditions and tried to make preparations, it was also obvious that he'd never been in space before. He had trouble keeping himself anchored while he worked.

"Who're you with?" Kevin asked. He had to talk much louder than he was used to; the low air pressure didn't carry sound very well. Although there were people in the compartments on either side and the partition was only thin nylon, they couldn't understand the conversations in the next cabins.

"Interplanet." Norsedal continued working with glue and Velcro. The glue smell was strong, but not excessively so. "I hope the air system doesn't have trouble with this," Norsedal said. "I suppose I should have brought water-soluble glue. But I wanted it to dry quickly. Maybe we should ask someone—"

"I wouldn't worry about it," Kevin said. Interplanet, he thought. That was the Zurich-based international consortium that maintained one of the two bases on Ceres. Kevin couldn't picture Jacob Norsedal as a miner or prospector and he certainly wasn't any kind of construction worker. "What will you be doing on Ceres?"

"Computer programming. And experiments with the computer system," Norsedal said. "Storekeeping—I'm supposed to set up an inventory control system for them. And work time-effectiveness studies. Anything that needs doing with computers." He seemed very happy about the idea.

"I—" Kevin hesitated. He didn't want to offend the man. Presumably there would be an opportunity to swap cabinmates once the ship was under way, but in any event there was certainly no sense in getting into an argument with someone you'd have to live with for months. His curiosity got the better of him. "You don't seem like a spaceman."

Norsedal smiled through his beard. "No. That's what the company said when I applied. It took me a long time to convince them. But look at it this way. A ten-year supply on insulin doesn't weigh very much. Nor does it matter if I'm overweight, not in Ceres' gravity, or in none at all. And I had one very good argument: I wanted to go and I can do the work." He began stowing his gear as he glued fuzz onto it. Decks of magnetic-backed cards. Three wargaming books. When he came to those he looked thoughtfully at the reader screen.

"I think I can tie that into my computer," Norsedal said. "We can use it for a display. Are you interested in wargames?"

Kevin had never thought about it. "After a few months in space I expect I'll be interested in anything—"

Norsedal grinned. "That's what I thought. We'll teach this thing to play Star Trek." He reached out to the screen and touched it, petting it like a dog: nice screen. Pat, pat.

* * *

They had two days aboard *Wayfarer* before the final boost toward Ceres. Kevin thought it would have been fun if there hadn't been so many people crowded aboard. He learned to eat in free fall, although he still managed to get a lot of the food into the intake grid of the air recirculation system: the only way to spoon food from plastic bags to mouth was in one smooth motion, never stopping. If he halted the spoon on its way, the food kept going to splatter against his face or shoot over his shoulder.

He also learned to do tumbling in zero-gravity. One of the other passengers organized a pool: the winner would be the first passenger to go in a single leap from A deck all the way to the aft bulkhead. No one looked like winning it just yet; four decks was the record. It was Kevin's turn to try when Captain Greiner ordered all the passengers back to their cabins for boost.

Weight felt strange. The ship boosted at about

ten percent of Earth's gravity, but Kevin found that quite enough. All over the ship loose objects fell to the decks.

"Last chance." Jacob Norsedal said. "Until halfway there. Anything lost after this boost is done will either go to the air intake grid, or it won't show up at all."

Ninety minutes later the acceleration ended. *Wayfarer* was now in a long elliptical orbit that would cross the orbit of Ceres. Left to itself, the ship would go on past, more than halfway to Juptier, before the Sun's gravity would finally turn it back to complete the ellipse and return it to its starting point. In order to land on Ceres, the ship would have to boost again when it got out to the orbit of the asteroid.

There would also be minor course-correction maneuvers during the trip, but except for those the ship's nuclear-pile engine wouldn't be started up until they arrived at Ceres's orbit. Then the ship would accelerate to catch up with the asteroid. That wouldn't happen for nine months.

Nine months was a long time, Kevin had thought, but he was surprised at how quickly time passed. With only ten crewmen aboard, the passengers had to take turns working ship maintenance systems. Kevin was assigned to life support, with the job of cleaning out the sewage-processor. It wasn't his favorite work, but he learned a lot about the algae tanks and chemical processors that took human wastes, including exhaled carbon dioxide, and turned them into oxygen and food.

There were also large leafy plants: lettuce,

spinach, even watermelons and pumpkins. These vegetables furnished variety in their food, but were not really important to the ship's ecology. It takes a lot of surface area to absorb sunlight enough to convert a hundred people's wastes, and the larger the plants the less surface they had for the mass they took up. Algae are not as pretty as strawberry plants, but they are highly efficient.

The heart of the system was a series of large transparent tanks filled with green water and tropical fish. Once *Wayfarer* was under way the crew erected large mirrors outside the hull. The mirrors collected sunlight and focussed it through plexiglass viewports onto the algae tanks. A ventilation system brought the ship's air into the tanks as a stream of bubbles. Other pumping systems collected sewage and forced it into chemical processors; the output was treated sewage that went to the algae tanks as fertilizer.

Kevin called it the "green slime works" and was always suspicious of the food served aboard *Wayfarer;* harvesting and food processing was somebody else's job, and Kevin didn't want to know the details. He knew that the algae became high-protein flour somewhere along the line—but he also knew what the algae tanks took in. The thought wasn't particularly appetizing.

He got to know most of his fellow passengers. Ellen was roomed with two other women in a slightly larger cabin on L Deck, not far from the stern. Wiley Ralston was one deck above her. So was Bill Dykes, the miner/prospector Kevin had met on the plane to Baja. Kevin met a number of others as well; he had a very popular roommate.

Jacob Norsedal was madly teaching his personal computer to play Star Trek, Galactic Empire, Waterloo, Alexander the Great, Diplomacy, and any other game people wanted to indulge in. He had also invented a three-dimensional interstellar war game with a dozen mutually opposing sides and that seemed destined to be interminable—the players needed a computer just to tell them their options. Norsedal didn't play games himself, but he loved being referee, and his quarters tended to be a meeting place for those with nothing to do.

Kevin, to his sorrow, wasn't included in that category. On his second day after boost a large man came to the stateroom. "Kevin Senecal?" he demanded.

"Me," Kevin admitted.

"George Lange. Senior Daedalus employee aboard. I guess I'm your boss." Lange held out a stack of casettes. "You're supposed to study these."

Kevin opened them warily. "That's a lot of reading—"

"It's just a start," Lange said. "I've got a lot more for you. You're expected to *learn* something on this trip." He glared at Norsedal's computer, which was marching armies across the reader screen. "There's *work* waiting out in the Belt."

"And we've got *months*," Wiley Ralston said. He came into the stateroom. With four people inside it was crowded, but not badly: Ralston and Norsedal took places near where the ceiling would have been if there had been a floor and ceiling; with no gravity, there was no up or down and any part of the room was as comfortable as any other.

"There's months' worth of learning to be done." Lange growled. "Look, this ship is *it*. Either we make some profits out of the Belt, or there won't be more ships going. Not even the big companies can keep up this investment without some return. So at least you, Senecal, will get to work learning what you ought to—"

Later Kevin found he had tapes on general space operations, mining, prospecting, environmental control systems, composition of asteroids, orbital mechanics—

Norsedal helped him study. He claimed to be interested, but Kevin thought Norsedal had probably learned everything on the tapes and was too polite to admit it. Certainly he was a good coach. Anything that could be done with a computer particularly interested him, and he showed Kevin how to do simple programs to solve most of the problems on the tapes. Slowly Kevin found himself learning what he had to know, even though it left him very little time for social life. His studies tended to keep him busy, so that he conversed mainly with Norsedal.

Three weeks out Kevin finished the first stack of tapes. "I suppose he'll have more," he said.

Norsedal was sitting yoga-fashion on nothing. He looked like a bearded Buddha. "Probably."

"So I don't tell him I'm done," Kevin said. He waved at the stack of tapes. "Cripes, according to that stuff we've licked all the problems, but every time I see Lange he gives me this bit about how desperate everything is, and how much work there is to do—" He stopped because Norsedal wasn't amused and it showed. "Are things that bad? I thought we knew how to live in space—"

"We do," Jacob said. "Technical capabilities exceed requirements by an order of magnitude. But Lange is right all the same. The space colonies aren't self-sufficient, and there aren't many ships. The Luna people want more Earth cargoes, the O'Neill Colony people want the ships, and the big companies can't afford to keep sending ships out to the Belt unless they get something back. I wouldn't be surprised if this were the last ship from Earth until the Ceres refineries prove they can make a profit."

"You mean it's *really* up to us?" Kevin asked.

Norsedal was very serious. "It might be. It's worse than that, really. Earth is so near the edge that if this attempt doesn't make it we may never be able to afford asteroid colonies again."

It was a sobering thought. Kevin looked at the pile of tapes. "I guess I'd better tell Lange I'm ready to get back to work."

VIII

With 130 people packed into quarters that would have been cramped for half that number it was inevitable that the passengers would get on each other's nerves. Kevin was surprised at just how few fights developed. There were plenty of quarrels and screaming matches, but not many blows. The worst part of it was the almost complete lack of privacy aboard *Wayfarer*.

For the first weeks this was no great problem for Kevin: there was too much to do. He had tapes to study, Norsedal's wargames, extravehicular activity practice under supervision of the crew, maintenance duties and other ship's work that was rotated among the passengers—and just plain getting used to living in zero-gravity.

He spent hours playing with liquids: squirt a dollop of colored water from a syringe, and it immediately became a sphere like a miniature planet. Inject an air bubble into it with a syringe and it assumed a new shape. Blow on it gently to get it rotating and it became a donut of water hanging in space.

There were rivers of stars to see outside any viewport. He had to learn the constellations all over again; there were just too many stars to let him recognize the old familiar patterns as seen from Earth, so many stars that in a darkened room you could almost read by starlight. But during EVA practice, perched above the ship's telescope tower with nothing ahead or above, he felt as if he were suspended motionless in space, a part of the universe. Kevin was always sad when his time was up and another passenger took his place. He eagerly looked forward to his practice sessions outside the ship, and wondered whether, when he reached the Belt and he would be outside for many hours at a time, he would ever get used to the wonder and grandeur of space. He hoped he would not.

As weeks went by, though, he found the lack of privacy becoming more irritating. There were 30 women among the 120 passengers aboard *Wayfarer*. Half of those were married and most of the remainder had formed quasi-permanent attachments. None of this bothered Kevin, since Ellen MacMillan remained at large and seemed to enjoy his company; but he could never be alone with her, and that *was* annoying.

Eventually the problem solved itself: they were assigned to environment systems maintenance during the same shift. Dismantling and cleaning sewer pipes wasn't his idea of a romantic setting, but it did have the advantage that no one else was interested in being in the same compartment while they worked. Felipe Carnel, the ship's Chief Engineer, was happy enough to leave the work to qualified passengers once he'd checked them out; and Ellen was as competent and conscientious as he.

The work was not demanding, merely messy and difficult; they had plenty of time to talk. For some reason Ellen seemed genuinely interested in Kevin and kept drawing him out. She was easy to talk to, and he found himself telling her about his early life, about school, and why he had come to space. Although he was usually somewhat shy with girls it was easy to be friends with Ellen.

"I think I've told you everything there is to know about me," he said finally. "And I don't know anything about you. You never talk about yourself—"

"Nothing to talk about." She squinted up at him and made a face. During the week they'd worked together they'd developed a system of signals. This one meant that she had sweat in her eyes and filth on her hands.

Kevin took a clean tissue and wiped her face. "Thanks." She went back to reaming out the plastic pipe.

"Come on," Kevin said. "You've made me do all the talking."

"There really isn't anything to tell," Ellen said. "I don't have any relatives. I was raised in an orphanage—"

"I didn't think they still had those," Kevin said. "Foster parents and—"

Ellen shuddered. "I was through several of those foster homes. Horrible way to live. Kevin, did you ever hear of the Futurian Foundation?"

"No."

"I guess not too many have. It's an organization that's interested in where—" She laughed. "It sounds silly if you're not a part of it."

"No, please. Tell me."

"Well, we're trying to look at where mankind is going," Ellen said defiantly. "Governments look ahead as far as the next election. The big corporations can look a little farther, sometimes as far as ten years. And nobody worries about what's going to happen after that. Nobody except us. We try to look hundreds, even thousands of years ahead."

"And you're a member of that—"

"Sort of. They raised me. When I was fifteen they bought me from the foster parents I was with —"

"Bought you? Sounds like slavery."

She shrugged, a tiny wriggling motion; they had all learned new gestures for use in zero-gravity. She shifted her location, wedging one foot under a pipe clamp so that she could use both hands for the job she was doing.

"In a way it is," she said. "The state pays the foster parents to raise orphans. It's profitable work. They're paid by the number of kids in their home, so the foster parents don't want to let anyone go. The social welfare people don't want to let you go either—if they don't have orphans to take care of, they can't justify their jobs. So the Futurians had to pay off the foster parents, some lawyers, and two social workers. I'm glad they did."

Kevin looked puzzled. Ellen laughed. "Nothing mysterious about it. They have a testing program to catch the right people young and get them thinking about the future instead of themselves. That's all there is to it. I've been brought up to be satisfied with enough to live on, not to want anything more except my work—so I've got everything I want."

"And you think that's not interesting?" Kevin said. "You seem to have found the secret of the ages."

She laughed again. It was a pleasant sound, even muted as it was by the low air pressure. "We don't keep all our recruits, you know. Most of the kids we bring up go off to normal lives. Only a few of us join the Fellowship."

"But you did?" She nodded. "I suppose that's like a priesthood," Kevin said.

His voice had betrayed his thoughts, and she laughed again. "Not really. We're not celibate, you know! Although sometimes you act as if you think I am—"

"Hey, wait a minute, that's not fair," Kevin protested.

She was laughing again. "The way conditions are on this ship we both might as well be monks— either that or adopt the attitude of monkeys in a zoo, and I'm afraid I haven't got to that point yet. There. That's done. You tighten up the connections while I clean up." She looked down at her hands. "Yuk."

Kevin pushed away from the bulkhead and expertly floated over to the pipe assembly. He was proud of his hard-won ability to work in null-gravity conditions. He got one foot wedged into the pipe retainer and braced the other against a wire channel, leaving both hands free, and applied a big wrench to the pipes. The fittings turned hard, and everything took at least twice as long to do in zero-gravity as it would have on Earth. Finally he had it done. "You can turn on the pressure."

The system worked again, with no leaks, and Kevin nodded in satisfaction.

"Now. We're alone, and this is done, and—" He reached for her. She didn't resist.

"I think we'd better stop," she said, after a while.

"Why?"

"Because this isn't a very private place, and I am *not* a monkey in a zoo. The Leones may not mind putting on demonstrations for the other passengers, but I do—"

"Nobody ever comes here."

"Yes they do." She pushed away from him and caught a look at her reflection in one of the big plexiglass algae tanks. "I'm a mess. Ugly—"

"You're not."

"Thank you. But I am. So are you, for that matter. Our faces are all swollen up, our lips are chapped, *and* we're getting pimples."

"All true but all irrelevant," Kevin said. "We knew that would happen before we signed up for a long trick in zero-gravity."

"But I didn't think I'd look *this* awful."

"You look all right to me." He did a double somersault from his bulkhead and landed just next to her. He grinned and reached for her again.

"Kevin, please . . ." Finally, she pushed away again. "Please. That's enough."

"Not for me—"

"Not for me either, but it's still all we're going to do," she said. "And don't look like a hurt little boy. Kevin, I like you. That's just the trouble. If we —this wouldn't be just a shipboard romance. Kevin, I can't afford emotional involvements. We've both got too much to do when we get to Ceres."

"So we have work to do. There's more to life than work—"

"Sometimes. Kevin, once we get to Ceres we may never see each other again. It's not fair to either of us to—to get too attached to each other."

"I'll take my chances."

"You say that now because I'm the only girl available. You wouldn't if—if you knew what you'd be getting into. I'm not somebody you ought to know, Kevin. I shouldn't have teased you. I'm sorry. I get lonely too, and I forgot that we'll never just be two people—"

"What?" Kevin frowned. There was a strange expression on Ellen's face, a strange look in her eyes, and he didn't understand.

"There's so much you can't know," Ellen said. "Kevin, we're friends. Let's leave it at that." She turned away to stare at pressure and flow gauges. "I think we've got this working again, and I've got some writing to do." She left the compartment hurriedly.

Kevin wanted to follow her, but she moved too quickly, and there were people in the corridors outside. He came back to stare into the algae tanks.

Tropical fish swam through the thick plant growth. They had adjusted to lack of gravity and oriented themselves as if the light source were "up." They no longer seemed confused—but Kevin was, and he didn't like it.

"She said she liked me," he muttered to the fish. "And it's a long way to Ceres." He could comfort himself with that. It was a long way to Ceres . . .

A week later they were both transferred to other ship's duties, not together. Kevin saw her quite often, but never alone.

Kevin's new assignment was on the bridge. His partner was Wiley Ralston, and Kevin found himself telling his friend about his problems with Ellen.

Ralston laughed. "Persistence, old buddy. Persistence and propinquity. Girls aren't any different from guys. They get horny too. Give it time."

"There doesn't seem to be a lot else to do," Kevin said.

"Yeah. Well, you'll have more of 'em to go after when we get to the Belt."

True enough, Kevin thought. But he wasn't sure that was what he wanted. He wasn't sure what love was, or whether he believed in it, but he kept wishing Ellen were around so he could tell her things he'd just thought of, and made excuses to go find her.

Eventually they were back in the farms and alone; and this time when he kissed her she didn't run away. A long time later, when they could speak again, she said, very seriously, "Kevin, we don't talk about love or the future. We're together while we're on the ship. Nothing permanent; nothing lasts after we reach the Belt."

"Sure," he said; but he didn't believe her.

* * *

Kevin and Wiley Ralston had been assigned to the bridge again when the halfway course correction came. Captain Greiner was very casual about it. First he slaved the computer to the high-gain antenna, then took position and velocity readings from both Earth and Ceres. Finally he pointed the main telescope to the bright star Vega.

The ship's computer digested the information for a minute. Then it flashed ready lights.

"And this does it," Greiner said. He threw switches giving control of the ship to the computer.

A recorded voice sounded. "Now hear this. Stand by for thirty seconds of very low gravity. Low thrust for thirty seconds, commencing in one minute. Fifty-nine, Fifty-eight . . ."

"Almost as if the ship didn't need me at all," Captain Greiner said. "If it weren't for the maintenance, it wouldn't."

"But you can operate without the computer, while it can't work without you," Kevin said.

Greiner laughed. "Not hardly. Everything's got to be too precise. If we had plenty of fuel, sure, I could navigate by hand calculations; but not the way we're cutting it."

"So even out here the machine replaces man," Wiley Ralston said. "Well, the damned machines can't do everything for us. Some things still need people. Though I wonder just how long—"

Kevin looked at him quizzically. Wiley grinned. "Just so long as they need us a few more years," Ralston said. "Long enough to get rich. Then they can run the whole damned universe by computer."

The countdown ended, and they felt weight again. Not very much weight, about one percent of Earth's gravity; but it felt strange to have a permanent "up" and "down" again. Kevin had found that he could orient himself to think of any direction "above" his head as "up" in zero-gravity; since he was facing forward, he suddenly found himself lying on his back instead of standing. He found later that everyone in the ship had had the same problem.

"Ceres has gravity," Jacob Norsedal said after dinner. "Let's see, about forty centimeters a second —four percent Earth gravity."

"Just enough so you can't jump off," Ellen said.

"A lot more than that." Norsedal said. His voice was apologetic but firm. He was apologetic for disagreeing; but he was never uncertain about his facts. He took his belt calculator, the small one he always carried, and punched in numbers. "You couldn't jump more than about 125 feet straight up," he said. "Of course, you'd take a while coming down." Click-click. "Not so long, thirteen seconds. Half a minute for the round trip, up and back down again. Of course I've left out the mass of your suit and tanks. I could run it with those—"

"Never mind," Ellen laughed. She, like everyone in the ship, had found that if you asked Norsedal a question you often learned more than you wanted to know. "It's going to take getting used to all over again," she said. "Having things fall instead of just drifting around the way they do here. And I've gotten used to sleeping in zero-gravity."

They sat at the entrance to Kevin and Jacob's stateroom. One of the inevitable tumbling contests was going through the central well of the ship. Bill

Dykes, the miner Kevin had met on the airplane to Baja, spun past doing somersaults and counting loudly. "Ninety-seven!" he announced with a grin as he went past. He was still centered in the opening, and it looked likely that he'd get all the way to the stern bulkhead. That was no longer unusual; the contest had been won weeks before, and now the passengers were trying to set a record for the number of somersaults before touching walls or decks.

"Damn!" Hal Leone was in Kevin's stateroom playing a stellar wargame with his wife Jeannine. The game used ballistic calculations, and Hal had managed to get his ship into an unrecoverable situation; no matter what he did, it was going to crash into a star. His wife chuckled. What made it embarrassing was that Hal was a mathematician and his wife a physician—but she always won.

Others gathered on F deck. It was almost time for another session of Norsedal's monster twelve-sided game, and the players were assembling. Someone produced a bottle of vodka vacuum-distilled from green slime. Despite its evil source it had no unusual taste at all. The bottle passed around. There was more activity in the well; a twirling contest, men and women pirouetting in midair. Then Bill Dykes came tumbling back toward the bow, followed closely by his cabinmate and partner, Carl Lundgren. They were counting loudly.

"Happy hour," Ellen said.

Suddenly another man leaped across the opening. He collided heavily with Carl Lundgren.

"Look where you're going!" Lundgren shouted.

"Shove it," the other man said. Kevin recognized him: Frank Sales, a loner with a foul temper. Sales was going out to work as a miner. He was a short, almost dwarfish man, who compensated for his small stature with a constant program of exercises. All the passengers were supposed to take their turn with the exercise machines, but Sales was the only one who took extra time on them as a matter of course.

"Goddamit, I was headed for a record," Lundgren said. "What'd you want to do that for?"

Sales grunted and turned away.

"I asked you a question!" Lundgren shouted. "Come back here."

"Hey, buddy," Bill Dykes said, grabbing Lundgren's arm, "Drop it. He ain't worth it."

Lundgren shook Dykes off. "Keep out of this, Bill. That sawed-off little bastard never looks where he's going. Who the hell does he think he is?"

"Are you talking about me?" Sales grasped a stanchion and turned back toward Lundgren. "Are you?"

"Damn right, you little creep."

"Hey—" Dykes protested, but it was too late. Sales dived toward Carl Lundgren and knocked him from his perch against the edge of F Deck. The two men became a tangle of arms and legs tumbling in the central well. Lundgren caught Sales by the hair and pulled; the result was that both tumbled out of control.

Others moved to try to separate them, but only

added to the tangle. Someone began to laugh and others joined. Ellen giggled. Then Sales's hand moved to his tool belt.

"Look out, Carl, the little bastard's got a knife!" Dykes shouted.

Lundgren turned frantically toward Sales. One of the others trying to separate them grabbed at Lundgren, missed, and caused him to spin violently again. Three other passengers dove toward the fighting men, and there was another wild tangle of bodies. Then bright blood spurted out to hang in large droplets in the air. It was impossibly red, tiny red planets hanging in space.

Someone screamed, more passengers and a crewman appeared to separate the fighters. When the two were pulled apart they saw that Carl Lundgren spurted blood in rythmic pulses from a slash across his throat.

"You've killed my partner!" Dykes roared. He started for Sales, but other passengers held him.

"He came for me!" Sales shouted. "You saw it, he ran right into me, I never meant to hurt him."

There was a babble of voices. "Get him to sick bay!" "Hold on to that murdering son of a bitch!" "Jeez, little buddy, you're going to be all right, you gotta be—" "Get a doctor!"

Jeannine Leone came out of Kevin's cabin and dove to the group holding Lundgren. Her hands worked frantically at the wound. "I can't get a grip," she said. "You, hold him against the deck. One of you hold onto my feet. Not like that! Hold me steady, I have to get pressure on this—"

Blood continued to stream into the ship. Bright

crimson spheres floated toward the air intake grid. "We need weight," Jeannine shouted. "Send for the Captain—"

"I'm here," Greiner said.

"We need weight. Not much, just enough to let me do steady work. Can you give us acceleration?"

"No," Greiner said. "Can't do it."

"But he'll die—"

"I hope not, but we can't do it!" The Captain's face was grim. "If we accelerate now we won't get to Ceres at all."

Jeannine continued working, but finally she straightened and shook her head. "Too late," she said. "He's dead. I don't know if I could have done anything even if we had gravity." She turned to Bill Dykes. "I'm sorry—"

"Not your fault," the miner said. He looked at his partner's body, then at Frank Sales. "Now we got a murderer to deal with. I say we put him outside now and get it over with."

IX

"Trial! We gotta have a trial," someone shouted. The Captain agreed. Eventually it was settled. Of course everyone wanted to watch.

There was no place aboard *Wayfarer* large enough to assemble the entire ship's company. The wardroom deck could hold about half of them, with people perched around the walls and hanging onto the deck above. The rest had to scatter through the central well. Since it wasn't possible to understand what was said from more than ten feet away, Captain Greiner had everyone put on their helmets and tune to a common channel. Eventually everyone was settled, some scattered all through the ship, others on the wardroom deck. It was not an orderly meeting.

"There are few precedents," Captain Greiner said, "but this isn't the first murder in space. I am not sure the previous cases apply, however. In the first space murder the satellite commander tried the case himself, and himself executed the murderer. Although the commander—it was Aeneas MacKenzie, by the way—offered to employ the entire satellite crew as jury, there were complications including threats against the families of crew members, and MacKenzie ended by acting alone.

"However, in that case there was no doubt about the guilt of the murderer, or that the crime was premeditated; the murder was part of a scheme to sabotage the satellite. Few have questioned the justice of MacKenzie's actions."

Kevin felt Ellen shudder.

"What's the matter?" he asked.

"Nothing," she said; but her voice was low and tightly controlled.

"This is farcical," someone shouted. Kevin couldn't tell who it was; the voice came through his headphones. "You can't even establish that there's *been* a murder, and there is no impartial jury. Everyone here is prejudiced."

"Who the hell is that?" Bill Dykes thundered. "Not been a murder? My partner's dead, and this bastard did it, and what's there to talk about? Put him outside and get it over with!"

Someone else shouted, "I got no use for Sales, but we have to let him tell his story—"

"Sure," Dykes said. "We listen to him, *then* we put him outside!"

Everyone began to talk at once. "It was a goddam accident—" "What the hell, fair fight—" "Damn murderin' bastard never was any use—"

"Silence," Greiner said. His voice carried authority. "We are holding this meeting to determine what we shall do. It will not become a shouting match."

"There's plenty of precedent from sailing ship days," someone said. "You can do anything you think best for the welfare of the ship."

"I am aware of that," Captain Greiner said. "As most of you know, I am an engineer and aircraft pilot by training. I do not come from a navy tradition and I must say I am reluctant to assume supreme authority—"

"You have to," someone shouted.

"But if that is what is needed, I will do so," Greiner finished.

Someone jumped up through the well to land in front of Captain Greiner. "I'm Martin Pacifico," he said. "I'm a lawyer."

There was a chorus of boos and hisses. "Who needs *him*?" Bill Dykes shouted.

It didn't seem to bother Pacifico. "Captain Greiner, the essence of a fair trial is an impartial jury. Obviously there is no possibility of such here. Even if there had been—and most of the passengers were witnesses to the alleged crime and thus were already not competent as jurors—your insistence on discussing this matter before the entire ship's company has contaminated all possible veniremen—"

"Oh, shut up!" Dykes yelled. "Captain, get that yo-yo out of here. My partner's dead, and dammit —"

"Enough," Captain Greiner said. "Mr. Pacifico, are you suggesting we wait until we reach Ceres to hold the trial?"

"That won't do either," Pacifico said. "Ceres has no jurisdiction—"

"So we must wait until Sales is returned to Earth?" Greiner asked. "Which could be ten years, or could be never—"

"Shut that goddam lawyer up," Dykes yelled. There were other shouts of agreement.

"May I speak?"

Kevin didn't recognize the newcomer, but Greiner evidently did. "Yes, Mr. Harwitt?" the Captain said.

"Harwitt?" Kevin asked.

"The Westinghouse supervisor," Ellen said. They spoke without using their microphones.

"Captain," Joe Harwitt said. "My company has an interest in this matter. Lundgren had signed up to work for us in the Ceres refinery and we paid for his passage. But now we have no one to do his work. I think that Sales owes us restitution."

"That is a civil matter," Pacifico said. "Not under consideration here. I would be glad to represent you, though—"

"Oh, shut up," Harwitt said. "I don't want money damages ten years from now, I want a refinery worker! It is too late to bring someone else out to take his place, but we can get *some* use out of Sales. He will have to do."

"I say, wait a moment—"

Captain Greiner seemed resigned. "Yes, Dr. Vaagts. I expected to hear from you sooner or later."

"Sales is signed up with Rheinmettal," Vaagts said, "and we will need him. You can't take him for Westinghouse—"

"Does Rheinmettal stand responsible for his actions?" Harwitt demanded. "You brought him here."

"Don't be ridiculous."

"I'm not being ridiculous. *Somebody's* got to

compensate Westinghouse for the loss of our worker. I say we have a right to Sales as replacement for Lundgren."

"But he would be of little use to you," Vaagts said. "You admit he is untrained for refinery work. But he has a good record in deep mining operations, and we can use him. Suppose, Joseph, that we keep him working for us, and compensate you for Lundgren's passage with funds withheld from his pay?"

"Rather have a worker than money," Harwitt said. "But I suppose we could make a deal. You'd have to pay interest, of course."

"I think that can be agreed," Vaagts said.

"You are speaking of slavery!" Pacifico shouted.

"Damn it, what about my dead partner?" Dykes demanded. "And his family back on Earth?"

"Ah," Vaagts said. "I suppose restitution to Lundgren's family is in order as well—we will divide Sales's pay between Westinghouse and Lundgren's family—

"Slavery," Pacifico said again.

"You can't do this to me," Sales shouted.

Everyone began talking at once. "Civil rights—" "Screw his rights—"

"Put the bastard outside and get it over with," Dykes said again. He didn't sound so positive now. "Only—maybe it's not so bad, making him pay—"

"We still have not established Mr. Sales's legal obligation to *anyone,*" Pacifico said.

"Captain, may I respectfully request," Dr. Vaagts said, "that if that extremely unpleasant lawyer person does not keep silent so that interested parties can come to agreement, we put *him* outside—"

"And who'd pay Interplanet compensation for losing Pacifico?" someone asked.

"Take up a collection?" another voice added hopefully.

"Let us first determine who are the interested parties," Captain Greiner said. "First, of course, Mr. Sales himself."

"Glad you jokers realize I'm still here," Sales said.

"Shut up," Dykes yelled.

"Second," Captain Greiner continued, "the relatives and friends of Mr. Lundgren. Certainly they must have a voice in any settlement. Third, the two companies: Rheinmettal, which employs Sales and has paid for his passage; and Westinghouse, which has lost the services of Mr. Lundgren. Are there any others?"

"Justice!" Pacifico said loudly.

"If all interested parties are satisfied then justice has probably been served," Greiner said. "Now: Mr. Dykes, what do you propose?"

"Put him out—only I'll say this. If Carol Lundgren and the kids can get something out of this, that'd be better. Won't do them any good if we space this little creep."

"So. And we have heard the proposals of the interested firms," Greiner said. "It now remains to hear from Mr. Sales himself. Sales, you are charged with murder. How do you plead?"

"It was a goddam accident—"

"We can, if you like, call witnesses and determine just what happened." Greiner said. "But I think we already know. There was an argument. You began a fight. You were losing it, and for whatever reason you drew a weapon which you used to menace Mr. Lundgren. Do you disagree so far?"

"Well—I just wanted to make him stop beatin' on me," Sales said. "I didn't intend to hurt him! You all saw it, somebody pushed him, he fell into my knife. I didn't go after him."

"I do not dispute that," Greiner said. "Does anyone?"

There were murmurs, but no one spoke up.

"About the way I saw it," Kevin said. Ellen nodded.

"The fact remains that you drew the weapon and menaced Mr. Lundgren with it, and thus you are the responsible party. You also began the fight."

"He provoked me—"

"But you struck the first blow."

"Fair fight's no murder," someone said.

"Perhaps," Greiner said. "But this was hardly a fair fight, with one party armed and the other not warned. I do not say what I would do if there were a formal duel aboard my ship, but I do say this was not a fair fight as I understand it. Have we established the facts to everyone's satisfaction?"

"This is terrible procedure," Pacifico shouted.

Greiner ignored him. "Then, Mr. Sales, you are certainly guilty of manslaughter. Do you dispute that?"

"He provoked me," Sales insisted.

"And you are accordingly found guilty of that charge," Greiner said. "We have no jail facilities aboard this ship, and it is not my job to provide punishment in any event. I sentence you to forfeiture of all pay and allowances for five years. You will continue to be employed by Rheinmettal, which will take sufficient measures to prevent your injuring anyone else, and your pay will be divided equally between the family of your victim and the company which employed him. So ordered. First Officer, write it into the log and I'll sign it. Dr. Vaagts, I deliver this man into your care. The ship's company is dismissed.

* * *

The rest of the trip to Ceres was uneventful—until the last day.

Kevin had once again been assigned to bridge duties, which consisted mostly of keeping the Captain and First Officer company, and making coffee in free fall—not the easiest job Kevin had ever done.

The last phase of the voyage was to be an acceleration lasting nearly three hours. *Wayfarer* was in a long elliptical orbit that crossed that of Ceres; in order to land on the asteroid it would be necessary to both change the ship's direction and to catch up with the tiny planet. The process began hours before the burn, with *Wayfarer's* electronic gear getting a precise position and velocity fix. The ship had to be located precisely with relation to Ceres.

Captain Greiner programmed the radar antenna to seek out the beacon signal from Ceres. "Here goes," he said. He pressed the keys to initiate the position fix, then reached for a squeeze-bottle of hot coffee. He squirted coffee into his mouth, swallowed, and looked back at the control board. Then he frowned. "What the devil?"

"Sir?" First Officer Leslie Seymour floated over to the Captain's station.

"I'm not getting anything," Greiner said. "Nothing at all."

"That's odd," Seymour said. "It's as if the antenna wasn't working. Maybe I'd better have a look—"

"Maybe you had, Mister."

Seymour was already wearing his pressure suit. He reached for his helmet.

"SHUTDOWN. WARNING. COMPUTER SHUTDOWN," the computer announced.

"The hell you say!" Greiner muttered. He turned to the ship's computer and examined displays. "Damn! Leslie, it says it has a power interrupt!"

"Jeez. Antenna not working and now the computer's going out—"

"Check out the antenna," Greiner ordered. He lifted his intercom microphone. "Chief Engineer! Mister Carnel, get up here on the double. Something's happened to the computer. Leslie, on your way, now."

"Yes, sir," Seymour left the bridge, headed for the main airlock.

"What's happening, Captain?" Kevin asked. "Is there something wrong with the computer?"

"Damned wrong," Greiner said. "And we can't possibly make rendezvous with Ceres without it— there you are, Felipe. Look at this thing!"

Felipe Carnel looked at the shutdown message, then opened a panel and stared at dials. "It says that regulated power's been cut off, Skipper," he said.

"Regulated power? Where the hell's *that* power supply?"

"Back aft," Carnel said. "It's never given any trouble before."

"Better go have a look," Greiner said.

"Rojj." Carnel turned to leave the bridge.

"And have a look at the seals on the cargo hold," Greiner said thoughtfully.

The engineer looked back quickly. There was astonishment and worry in his voice. "Sir, you don't think—"

"Mister, I don't know what to think. Just check things out."

"Aye aye, sir." Carnel left hurriedly.

"Sir?" Kevin asked. "I thought we got power from the reactor."

"We do," Greiner said. "And there's no problem with the main power system. You can see that—the ventilation system's working, the lights are on. Nothing wrong there. But the brain here eats a very precise diet. It wants 400 cycle power, and that doesn't mean 399.9 either. If the brain's not getting what it wants, it shuts down to avoid damage to itself." Greiner frowned. "In fact, I wonder if it's not reporting antenna problems when all that's wrong is the power supply? We'll find out." Greiner didn't seem very worried.

It didn't seem serious, and Kevin went back to making more coffee. After all, they had ten hours before they started the engine. Besides—he could *see* Ceres in the ship's main telescope. He had watched it grow from a point to a recognizable object, no details but definitely a disc. They could aim for it and blast—

First Officer Seymour came back onto the bridge. "The antenna's gone, Skipper."

"Gone?"

"Clean gone. Like it was sawed off, or maybe blasted off with a couple of turns of prima-cord. Gone, anyway."

"Bat puckey. It can't be gone," Greiner said. "Blasted off? Sabotage?"

"Looks like it to me," Seymour said.

"Hmm. Well, we can still navigate with the telescope. If we get the computer running again," Greiner said. "But if—you really think it was sabotage, Leslie?"

"Yes, sir. What else could it be?"

They waited in silence. Finally Kevin asked, "If the computer's really out, what happens?"

"We don't get to Ceres," Greiner said. His voice was grim.

"Three years to home," Seymour added. "If we're lucky we can cut some off that, but not a lot. Think this tub will keep us alive for three more years, Skipper?"

"It might. With a lot of work," Greiner said. He looked thoughtful. "Present orbit takes us out to better than three and a half AU before we head back toward Earth. Less than ten percent of the sunlight we get down near Earth. It'd be close for a while. Not much light for the ship's farm."

"But—I can *see* Ceres," Kevin protested.

Greiner laughed without humor. "Sure. But how much do I burn aimed in what direction? Kevin, we've got just enough fuel aboard to set us down on Ceres. Nothing to spare for mistakes. Without the ship's computer we could never do it—"

"Can we get back to Earth without the computer?" Kevin asked.

"No. But that's not the problem. It's only the power supply. If we have to we can build another. We can build another antenna, too—ah." He stopped as Felipe Carnel came back into the bridge compartment. "Well?" Greiner demanded impatiently.

"Cargo seals are all intact," Carnel said. "I put Phelps on watch down there, just in case—"

"Phelps alone?"

"No, I asked three passengers, random selection, to stand watch with him."

"Good," Greiner said. "And the power system?"

"Blown to hell," Carnel said. "Somebody put about fifty grams of plastique into the system. Messed it up good."

"And the spare is gone," Greiner said quietly.

"Might as well be. Been taken apart into little bits."

"How long to rebuild?" Greiner demanded. His tone indicated that he already knew the answer.

"Days," Carnel said. "Three or four days anyway."

"By which time we'll be long past Ceres and headed out to nowhere," Greiner said. "Interesting. Someone put a lot of thought into this. He's sabotaged the exact two systems to keep us from landing on Ceres without actually crippling the ship."

Greiner's calm broke at last. "That son of a bitch! He's done it! I can't put the cargo on Ceres —" he shouted.

"And there may never be another ship out here again," Felipe Carnel finished for him. "Somebody's just damned near killed the whole asteroid mining business."

X

"There must be something we can do." First Officer Seymour pounded his fist into his palm. "Raise Earth and have them run off the problem in Zurich—"

"Without the high-gain antenna?" Felipe Carnel laughed. "We can't raise Earth without that antenna."

"Ceres, then," Seymour said. "They've got a big computer—"

"And no programs," Captain Greiner said. "And once again, without the antenna, we can't rely on communications with them. We'll try, but I've no confidence." Greiner looked at the last print-outs from the ship's computer. *Wayfarer*'s last known position was one hundred thousand kilometers from Ceres. The ship's orbit crossed that of the asteroid at a sharp angle; *Wayfarer* would have to change direction, then catch up; in practice that meant a smooth curve stretching from *Wayfarer*'s present course to the asteroid's orbit, with a slight change of orbit plane as well—and Ceres moves at eighteen kilometers each second.

The problem was not merely to get to Ceres, but to arrive with exactly the same velocity as the asteroid, and going in exactly the same direction. The navigation would be only slightly less complicated than hitting a BB in flight with another BB fired by a gunner who had bad eyesight. An error of a tenth of a kilometer per second would put the ship impossibly far away from its target.

"Leslie, try raising Ceres," Captain Greiner said. "Let's see if they have advice."

First Officer Seymour floated to the communications set and anchored himself to the stool. He lifted the microphone and began calling.

"What I want to know is *who*," Greiner said. "Damned clever chap, whoever it was. This was well planned. We keep our fuel, drift on in our ellipse, and eventually return to Earth. Stops us without committing suicide."

"But why?" Kevin asked.

Greiner shook his head. "Who'd benefit from this? Too many to count. The African mining outfits don't want competition from asteroid mines. Anti-technology people want to stop space exploration altogether—"

"Lunar mining outfits," Felipe Carnel cut in. "Or even the O'Neill colony people—they've been making noises about what a waste Belt operations are—"

"Skipper, I've got them, but they can't understand me," Leslie Seymour said. "OUR COMPUTER IS OUT," he shouted, then looked sheepish. "They just don't read us."

"Maybe when we get closer—" Kevin said.

"By then it will be too late," Greiner said. He stared at Kevin. "You look like a man with an idea. Have you thought of something?"

"Possibly, Captain, I know somebody who can compute the burn for us."

"Who? And how—"

"My cabinmate, Jacob Norsedal."

"Norsedal," Greiner said. "He's been up here a number of times. Very interested in our ship's brain. Yes, I'd say he knows computers, but this isn't a computer problem, Kevin. We cannot rebuild that power supply in the few hours we have left, and we don't need a program, we need a computer—"

"Yes, sir, but he's got his own," Kevin said.

"I've seen it," Greiner said "Kevin, he can't possibly do this calculation with that little belt model he carries—"

"I wouldn't bet on that," Kevin said. "But he doesn't have to. He's got a much bigger one in our cabin. Uses it for wargames. Recreation stuff. And he's been keeping track of *Wayfarer*. He calculated the midcourse correction you made, and said something about it being off, but not much—"

Grenier looked thoughtful. "Felipe, go ask Mr. Norsedal to come to the bridge. And ask him to bring that extra brain with him."

"Right," Carnel said.

"And you needn't tell the passengers about our problem," Greiner added. He waited until the engineer had left the control cabin. "Now. Kevin, how sure are you that Mr Norsedal isn't the one who bollixed our system to begin with? I wonder who else could have thought of this method?"

"You'd think that was funny if you knew

Jacob," Kevin said. "He's a space fanatic. Also a computer fanatic—he likes them more than he likes people. He'd never harm one."

"I point out to you that this one hasn't been harmed," Greiner said. "And I grant you it's not likely, but it's certainly possible that someone who seems to be a space fanatic could be one of the anti-technology people. They do study technological systems, you know."

"Possibly, but Jacob isn't against technology," Kevin insisted.

"I hope you're right."

* * *

When Carnel returned with Norsedal, Captain Greiner explained the problem. "Senecal here thinks you can do something," Greiner said.

"How much time do we have?" Norsedal asked.

"The burn was scheduled to take place in four hours." Grenier answered.

"Not much time." Norsedal looked thoughtful.

"No. Well, it was just a possibility. I didn't really believe in—"

"But I think we can do something," Norsedal said. He went over to the chart table and placed an attaché case on it, using the table straps to hold it in place. He anchored himself to the stool at the table, then opened the case and patted the computer inside. "Nice computer. Fortunately, I already have some of the programs we'll need. Now let's see—"

Jacob opened another compartment and took out paper. "Captain, I can program the course, but I can't possibly patch my computer into the ship's drive system—"

"No sweat," Felipe Carnel interjected. "We've got a lot of little special-purpose computers for that. One is slaved to the gyro system and controls the engine thrust. You tell the ship where to go and I'll see that she goes there."

"Good. I thought so," Norsedal said. "If you didn't have a lot of smaller computers dedicated to special purposes, the air system wouldn't work—" He began to work furiously. Pencils and paper floated away from him, to be retrieved by one of the others. He drank coffee constantly.

An hour went by. Then another. Finally Norsedal began punching input buttons.

"Done?" Captain Greiner asked.

"I have the basic program. Now we have to get it checked out and running," Norsedal said. He continued to type inputs. "Now we'll just try—"

He pressed buttons. There was a moment of silence, then the readout screen filled with numbers. "Stopped on an input error," Norsedal muttered. "That's simple enough." He typed for a moment, then looked up. "Captain, have you decided you will fly this course once I have it?"

"I'm still thinking about that," Greiner said. "No point in making decisions unless there's something to decide. Do you think you'll have it?"

"Probably." Norsedal didn't look up from his console. He muttered, sometimes to himself, sometimes to the computer. "Nice computer, tell me what I did wrong this time . . ."

"I don't like this much," Leslie Seymour said.

"Nor I," Greiner said. "But you know what happens if we do not deliver this cargo."

"Yes. I suppose we have to try." Seymour went

to the main telescope. "At least we can get decent bearings," he said. "There's Ceres, nice and clear—"

"I hope so," Norsedal said. "I had to compute the course as a function of the position of Ceres relative to Vega. We'll need constant sightings on both."

"We can get them," Seymour said. "Captain, maybe it wouldn't be a bad idea to protect the main telescope. Before that son of a bitch gets to it—"

"Good thinking," Captain Greiner said. "In fact, we ought to locate all the passengers and crew and set them to watching each other before there's more sabotage. I should have thought of that earlier." Greiner was apologetic. "I was never a ship captain, merely an astronaut with the European Space Program. Not the best training for what we're faced with. Leslie, see to it, will you?"

"Right, Skipper. Senecal, come with me, please. I want you to go outside and watch the telescope until we're certain that everyone is accounted for."

"Not alone," Greiner said. "Not that we don't trust you, Kevin—but who can we trust?"

"I understand," Kevin said. "May I use your intercom?"

"What for?"

"To call a friend." He went to the intercom panel and dialled a stateroom number. "Ellen, they've asked me to do an EVA. Will you come with me?"

"Who did you call?" Greiner asked.

"Ellen MacMillan. We've worked together on

other jobs in this ship, and I *know* she can take care of herself outside."

"I heard about your difficulty getting to *Wayfarer*," Greiner said. "Yes, I'd think MacMillan would be a good partner. Certainly we could trust her."

"But Skipper," Leslie Seymour protested. "We can't let *her* go outside—"

"Now that she's said she will, have you any way you can think of to stop her?" Greiner demanded.

And what is this all about, Kevin wondered. He had no time to ask.

Seymour sighed. "No. I don't suppose I can," he said. "I guess she'll do nicely. Let's go find her." He opened the companionway door.

There were three people waiting outside in the main corridor. One came in quickly, pushing past Seymour.

"Mr. Pacifico, what the devil are you doing on my bridge?" Captain Greiner demanded.

"I represent the passengers," Pacifico said. His voice, already garbled by the lower atmospheric pressure in the ship, sounded shrill and petulant. "We've been told that the main computer is out, and you're going to chance a landing on Ceres anyway."

"Who told you?" Felipe Carnel demanded.

"It's all over the ship," Pacifico said. He turned to the others who had come in with him. "Isn't it?"

"That happens to be the case," Dr. Vaagts said.

"I hadn't expected *you* to protest," Greiner said.

"Nor am I protesting," Vaagts said. "I merely wanted to know what is happening. Mr. Pacifico certainly doesn't represent me, or Rheinmettal."

"So who do you represent, Pacifico?" Carnel asked.

"Most of the passengers. We demand that we be consulted before you undertake a dangerous maneuver like this. Isn't it true that if you do nothing we'll go back to Earth, but if you try for Ceres and miss we'll have no fuel left? We'll all be dead?"

"True enough," Greiner said.

"And what confidence do you have in—you've got *him* doing it? The wargamer? Captain, you can't do this. You must take a vote—"

"Vote hell. Leslie, you and Senecal were going out to locate all the ship's company."

"Right, Skipper," Seymour said.

"And you, Pacifico, get off my bridge. Now. Or I'll have you thrown off."

"We have rights—"

"Leslie, heave him out."

"With pleasure, Captain." First Officer Seymour launched himself toward the lawyer.

"I'm leaving," Pacifico said. "But you haven't heard the last of this, Greiner. You are not a king, and this isn't the Eighteenth Century—" He went out quickly as Seymour prepared to take hold of him.

Kevin found Ellen in her cabin. He explained what had happened. "Finish getting into your suit," he told her. "We're supposed to go outside and look after the main telescope."

"Sure. You wait out in the corridor."

"Sure you don't need any help?"

"Thank you, no."

When they reached the airlock, Seymour had got most of the passengers together in the central well. A crewman guarded the airlock. Kevin and Ellen checked their air supplies, then went out as Seymour was calling the roll of the ship's company.

* * *

Wayfarer had two airlocks. One was right in the bows, a large docking port that allowed smaller space capsules to link up with the ship, and could also be used to link with an airtight corridor connecting the ship with the Ceres spaceport, or even with another ship. The other was a smaller personnel lock on the side of the hull just aft of the bows. Kevin and Ellen went out that way. There was a small ladder leading forward.

With no gravity they had to be careful not to drift away from the ship. It would be easy to jump entirely away from *Wayfarer*. Although they couldn't fall off—they were moving at the same velocity as *Wayfarer*, and would until the ship's engines were started up—if anyone became separated from the ship he would drift away forever, moving slowly out into space.

They climbed carefully to the forward end of the ship and rounded it. Now there was nothing ahead of them at all. *Wayfarer* floated among a river of stars, bright starlight and the black shadows of space, and there was no sense of motion at all. They hung in glory. The sun was behind the ship so that they were both in deep shadow, with just enough starlight so they could see each other. Their flashlights made small pools of light on the ship's dark hull.

"Magnificent," Kevin murmured. "I could stay here for the rest of the trip."

Ellen floated over to him and silently touched his gloved hand. It wasn't a moment for talking. They found places to anchor themselves and waited in silence. The big telescope was a few meters away. It moved slightly as Captain Greiner took sights.

Kevin searched for constellations among the stars. He could make out only a few of the traditional ones; there were too many stars, millions more than the ancient Babylonians who had named the constellations had ever been able to see.

"Now that our eyes are adjusted, we'd best have a look at the telescope," Ellen said.

"Right." They moved across the blunt bow of the spaceship. There were convenient handholds at intervals. *Wayfarer* would never enter an atmosphere and had no need for streamlining.

The telescope was large, over a foot in diameter, with flexible seals that let it pass through the ship's hull and into the control bridge. They moved next to it and examined it with their flashlights.

"That doesn't belong there." Ellen sounded very alm and not surprised. Her light indicated something about the size and shape of a coffee can. It was taped to the telescope barrel.

"It may go off anyway. When you move it," Kevin said. "Get away from it—"

"This is my job," she said. "Move back. Farther."

"No. You move—"

"I told you, it's my job. Now move or don't, I'm going to take this thing off."

Kevin felt like an idiot. He was afraid of the bomb, and he was also unwilling to move away to safety while Ellen worked on it.

"Idiot, somebody's got to tell them what happened," Ellen said. "If it goes off. So get away from here—"

"No."

"Stubborn idiot."

"No worse than you are—"

"True. There. I have it." She held up the can. "It didn't explode yet." She crawled toward the side of the ship, then got a firm grip on the handhold with her left hand. With her right she threw the can outward, away from the ship. They watched it dwindle and vanish into space. "Maybe it was old coffee grounds," she said.

"Maybe." Kevin found that he'd been holding his breath. "Ellen—what did you mean, it's your job?"

"I shouldn't have said that. I was scared. Kevin, please—forget that I said that."

"Sure," he said. But he knew he wouldn't.

XI

"Outside party, this is Seymour." The First Officer's voice was loud in Kevin's helmet phones. It seemed a grating irritation in the silent grandeur of space.

"We're here," Ellen answered. "We found a bomb—or something that looked like one—attached to the telescope."

"But when was it put there?" Seymour demanded. "I looked at the telescope when I checked the high gain antenna. I'm sure I would have seen anything—"

"I don't know, but it was there," Kevin said. "Ellen threw it off the ship about two minutes ago. It will be a kilometer away by now."

"More like a couple of hundred meters," Ellen said. "It's difficult to throw anything very hard. But I'm sure it's far enough."

"Good. That's not what I called you about," Seymour said. "There are two passengers missing."

"Who?" Kevin asked.

"George Lange and that Pacifico person."

"George?" Ellen was incredulous. "He couldn't possibly have had anything to do with sabotaging the ship."

"He's my boss," Kevin said. "Always trying to get me to work. Ellen's right, he's not the saboteur. Pacifico—well, he's another matter."

"I think you ought to have a look around," Seymour said. "But don't take long. We start the engines in ten minutes, and you'll have to be inside before that."

"We'll go in just before the burn," Ellen said. "Until then—somebody put that bomb on the telescope. We'll watch."

"Right. Out," Seymour said.

Ellen moved closer to Kevin. "Turn off your radio," she said. When he did, she put her helmet against his. "Do you have any kind of weapon?"

"Only the knife in my tool kit."

"I wish we had a pistol."

"But—there aren't any pistols aboard, no guns at all."

"How do you know?" she demanded. "Kevin, I'm worried."

"About Pacifico? He's a pipsqueak—"

"He seems to be. But if Lange is missing, someone killed him. He wouldn't have any reason to hide. He must have caught the saboteurs in the act, and they killed him."

Kevin tried to remember what little he knew about Lange. It wasn't much. He'd brought Kevin the tapes and made him study them, and he'd talked in a general way about the work Deadalus Corporation would be doing on Ceres. Nothing definite. "How can you be so sure it wasn't Lange who planted the bomb?" Kevin demanded.

"I'm sure. Kevin, I think we should separate. You go watch the port side, I'll watch the starboard. Burn is ten minutes from now. We have to keep anyone from getting up here during the next five minutes. Then we'll be safe; and we'll be able to put the cargo down on Ceres—"

She started to move away, but Kevin caught her and pulled her back until he could put his helmet against hers. "Be careful," he said.

"Sure."

And, he wondered as he crawled toward the port side of the ship, what the hell is that cargo? Captain Greiner talked about it. So does Ellen. Everyone seems to know but me . . . there had been one series of launch capsules that had been guarded by company police and Mexican Army tanks. What could be that valuable?

He reached the edge and looked along the ship, past the hydrogen tanks to the big ring at the end of the ship. Nothing moved. He wondered if he should show a light. If someone really wanted to cripple *Wayfarer,* it would only take puncturing a couple of those tanks.

But that would completely cripple the ship. It would be suicide for the saboteur, and so far whoever was doing this had been careful not to really damage *Wayfarer,* just put the ship out of operation for a few hours until it would be too late to get to Ceres.

If he could reach the telescope, though, he could still keep them from landing.

Lange. Could it have been George Lange? How likely that Pacifico could knock out the antenna and computer power supply? Or kill Lange? Pacifico wasn't much larger than Ellen, while Lange was bigger than Kevin. Not that that meant anything—

being large was no real advantage in free fall. It just meant long legs to bump into things. But Kevin doubted that Pacifico knew enough about the ship to have been the saboteur—

He glanced at his watch. Five minutes to burn: time to be getting inside. Even as he thought it, Seymour's voice came into his headset. "That ought to do it," the First Officer said. "Best get into the airlock. We're going to start rotating ship for the burn."

"Right, Ellen—"

"Kev, there's somebody out here with us!" Ellen shouted. "I saw him move. Just then. He's down by the tanks."

"Good Lord." Seymour sounded worried. "But we've got to start maneuvers. We can't stop now— the burn must be exactly on time—exactly!"

"I know," Ellen said quietly. "I'm going after him. Kevin, get inside."

"Don't be silly." He clawed his way over the bow of the ship as she vanished around the far side.

"Hang on," Seymour ordered. "In one minute and . . . three seconds we start turning ship. We have to."

"Right," Kevin answered. "Ellen. What's happening?"

There was no answer. He reached the place where he'd last seen her and looked aft down the length of the ship. There was a flash of light from down there somewhere. He went over, pulling himself along the ladder, trying to make sure he was always holding it.

"If you start the engines I'll puncture the tanks!"

came a high pitched voice. Pacifico's. He sounded determined. Afraid but determined. "I'll do it!" the lawyer shouted.

"But—why do you want to keep us from getting to Ceres!" Seymour asked.

"I don't care about that," Pacifico said. "I want to go to Ceres. But you won't get us there! You can't navigate this ship with a suitcase computer; you've no right to risk our lives that way!"

"If you puncture the tanks you'll kill all of us including yourself," Kevin said.

"No I won't. We don't need all the fuel to get back to Earth. Stay away from me! I'll do it—"

"We're turning," Seympur said.

The ship moved slightly as attitude jets fired. It rotated slowly. Kevin didn't find it hard to hang on, and then the counter-jets fired to stop the turn. The ship was now heading almost exactly away from Ceres.

Kevin reached the tankage complex. It was dark among the long hydrogen tanks. "Ellen," he called.

"I see you," she said. "I think he's straight ahead of you."

"Get away from me," Pacifico screamed. "I'll do it, I swear I will!"

Kevin moved further into the tankage complex. Pacifico's voice came from nowhere and everywhere; it was weird, hearing him but being unable to locate him by sound. Kevin wondered if the lawyer had seen him. He saw no one. Not Ellen, not Pacifico. "You idiot, all the tanks are connected together," Kevin said, "If you puncture one of them, you'll let all the fuel escape."

"I don't believe that," Pacifico said. "It

wouldn't make sense as a design. Meteoroids—"

"I'm afraid what Senecal is telling you is the truth," Seymour's voice interjected. "The tanks don't connect normally, but when we make preparation for using the main engines we have to interconnect them. Otherwise the fuel would be burned out of one tank at a time and we'd get off balance."

That makes sense, Kevin thought. I wonder if it's true? The important thing is to get Pacifico talking and keep him occupied until we find him. And then what? Kevin fingered the knife in his pouch. That seemed drastic—

"Kev! I've got him! Aft of where you are and around clockwise sixty degrees!" Ellen's voice came in panting gasps.

Kevin moved in the direction she'd indicated. He saw Ellen and the lawyer struggling like clumsy wrestlers, their bulky suits preventing either of them from getting a decisive hold.

"One minute to burn," Seymour said. "Can you get into the airlock?"

" 'Fraid not," Ellen said. "Maybe we'll be all right here among the tanks—" Her voice rose. "Kevin!" she shouted in terror.

Both of them had moved away from the ship. Somehow they'd both lost their holds on the ship while trying to fight each other, and now they drifted free, a few feet away, unable to get back.

"My God! Help!" Pacifico screamed.

"Burn in forty seconds," Seymour said.

"You can't!" Pacifico screamed. "It's inhuman! You'll kill us!"

"Can't delay," Seymour said.

And he means that, Kevin thought. Not that Ellen would want him to delay. The Belt operation means too much to her. It's up to me, now. He dove forward, through the tankage. His months of practice in somersaulting through the ship let him get through the tanks in a clean arc.

He caught the ladder at the last possible moment, and reached out toward Ellen. "Grab hold!" he called.

She reached for him, missed by inches. He stretched but couldn't catch her.

"Ten seconds," Seymour announced.

"We're drifting free of the ship!" Pacifico screamed. "You can't do this, you can't—"

Kevin grabbed the safety line on his belt and hooked it to the ladder, then, letting the reel run free, leaped out toward Ellen. He grabbed her with both hands, then grunted with relief.

"You damn fool," she said. "You'll kill yourself—"

"Three. Two. One. Ignite," Seymour said.

The ship's engines started. There was no sound and no flame. Hydrogen was pumped from the tanks and into the nuclear pile on its sting at the end of the ship. The nuclear reactor heated the hydrogen and forced it back through nozzles. The ship drove forward at a tenth of a gravity.

Kevin felt Ellen as a sudden dead weight. He threw in the stop on his belt reel, and they dangled from the ladder, with nothing holding them but the thin nylon line. Pacifico, still screaming, vanished behind as the ship drove forward.

As the ship moved, suddenly they and the safety

line formed a pendulum. They felt the acceleration as they would a tenth of Earth's gravity as centrifugal force moved them until they swung back and forth in a small arc directly beneath the ladder. Kevin painfully reached up, still holding Ellen's hand with his. She wasn't heavy, only a tenth of what her weight would have been on Earth, But Kevin wasn't used to *any* gravity. He held tightly, irrationally afraid that the thin nylon line wouldn't hold their combined weight of fifty pounds. He couldn't quite reach the ladder.

"Help! You can't leave me here to die in space! Help!" Pacifico screamed in terror. The ship moved inexorably away from him. Within thirty seconds he would be nearly half a kilometer behind, doomed to the loneliest death possible, alone in a river of stars and the emptiness of space.

"Can you let me down a little further?" Ellen asked. "I can almost reach one of the fuel pipes—"

"No hands." Kevin said. "I've—"

"Here. I've got you," Ellen said. "Now let us down a meter or so."

"How can you be so damned calm?" Kevin snarled.

He let go of her with one hand and reached the ratchet control on his belt line. He let the safety line run free for a second, then locked it again. They both fell toward the aft end of the ship, then were brought up short by the line. The thin nylon held easily.

"There. I've got it," Ellen said. "I've got my safety line clipped to the pipe support. Here—let out more of your line, and I'll pull you over."

Kevin did as he was told. Seconds later he had a purchase on one of the fuel pipes. He looked up— the forward end of the ship was *up* now, and that was strange, to have a definite up and down. The pipe supports formed a ladder of sorts. It wouldn't be hard to climb back to the regular ladder.

"I guess we're safe," Kevin said.

"Thank God," Seymour said. "You're sure?"

"Yes," Kevin said.

They could still hear Pacifico's screams. His signal was growing weaker as he fell farther and farther behind.

"Pacifico," Ellen called. "Who hired you to sabotage the ship?"

"I didn't do it," Pacifico's voice said. "You've got to come back for me! It's not too late, I can see you, please, my God. Please, please come back for me, I didn't do it, I only wanted to stop this mad—"

His voice faded in and out now. "Come back. Please come back, you can find me, please . . ."

Kevin felt Ellen shudder beside him. He put his arm across her shoulders and felt her trembling. "It's all right," he said. "We're all right now—"

She didn't answer. After a while she pointed up toward the ladder. They began to climb. It seemed to take forever to reach the airlock. They thought they heard the lawyer's screams, ever fainter, the whole time.

XII

The office was Aeneas MacKenzie's only real luxury. It had a real window of thick quartz that overlooked the barren landscape of the Moon, and beyond that the glory of Earth hung suspended in black velvet. He often sat at his desk and stared out at the fragile Earth, a small blue world wrapped in white wispy clouds. He had lived on the Moon for twenty years and would never return to the world of his birth; but he loved Earth, and he missed her.

So little time, he thought. So little time until—he broke off the thought, because he had a vivid imagination, and it would be all too easy to see the fragile Earth covered with pinpoints of brilliant light, lights that would shine more brightly than the Sun until they faded and the ugly mushroom clouds rose through Earth's clean garments.

It would be easy, too, to imagine that he could see beneath the clouds, watch men and women working their lives out to no purpose but continued misery and starvation. That was life now for all too many; in a few years the globe might be covered with people who had nothing left to hope for. Desperation might tempt them to anything.

There were faint sounds in the office: the whine

of the air system, the faint rumblings of his miners digging into the lunar regolith, other sounds of construction and expansion; the sounds of success, and they mocked him. The future of Diana Base, and of Earth, did not depend on lunar miners. It depended on hard-eyed men in dark suits who sat in Zurich board rooms; it depended on the man in the Oval Office in Washington, and another man in the Kremlin; but mostly it depended on events more than a hundred million miles away, and over those Aeneas had no control.

His reverie was interrupted by a voice in his head. It made no sound, and if there had been anyone in the room with him, they would not have heard it; the implanted transceiver fed directly into his nervous system, and took its instructions from his thoughts. He had lived with the implant for so long that it was part of him. He would have missed it if it did not work; but he had never liked it.

"THERE IS A MESSAGE FROM CERES," the voice said.

"IS SHE SAFE?" Aeneas thought. It was a ridiculous question; not even the base central computer had been given enough data to know who he meant. "CANCEL THAT QUESTION. HOW IS THE MESSAGE SIGNED?"

"HOT LIPS."

Thank God, Aeneas thought. He was careful not to think that into the computer. His prayers were not meant for a machine. "I WANT THE FULL TEXT AS A PRINT-OUT," he ordered. It would take a little longer, but he would rather read it than hear it. "DECODE AND PRINT. KEEP NO COPY IN MEMORY."

"ACKNOWLEDGED."

"ASK LAURIE JO TO COME TO ME."

—Pause—"DONE."

And now there was nothing to do but wait. He leaned back in the chair, smoothing his shock of white-gray hair with slender fingers. Even in Luna's low gravity he felt his years. He had been forty when he came to the Moon, and even though Lunar gravity did not age men as much as Earth's did, there had been little rest in the last quarter century. Not for Aeneas MacKenzie. Presently he began to doze. Images formed in his mind.

* * *

Economists once thought there could never be a period of both inflation and high unemployment. They were wrong. In the last third of the Twentieth Century both were normal conditions. With millions out of work, governments tried to buy their way to prosperity through deficit financing. They printed bonds and certificates and paper money and more paper money, and soon they were all worthless. Wages and prices spiraled. People who had saved all their lives found their savings worth nothing, less than nothing, and simply to live had to turn for aid to governments that had ruined them in the first place. The governments had to find more and more money, and the printing presses were cheap. The results were predictable, but no less disastrous for being so.

The democracies in particular faced an impossible dilemma. There wasn't enough money to fund both technological research and welfare programs. Technological research was expensive and directly employed comparatively few people. Soon the space programs were cut back, cut again, cut once more. Meanwhile the anti-technology movements gained recruits. "Only One Earth." "Alternate Technology." "Appropriate Technology." "Ecology." Those slogans and a dozen like them became watchwords, and space programs, energy research, electronics research, all began to die.

For a while private industries continued research programs, but soon the governments, desperate for more funds to spend on popular programs, raised taxes so high that there was nothing left for risk investment. The companies cut back as had the governments; especially so as the consumer advocates forced the corporations to accept consumer representatives on their boards of directors, and the consumer representatives were almost universally dedicated against technology and technological "fixes."

Then the United States was rocked by a series of scandals. Watergate began it, but the scars from that had not healed before another scandal emerged, and another after that. The People's Alliance rose to displace the traditional political parties, and swept into Washington as an irresistible reform movement. Its leader, Greg Tolland, and his manager, Aeneas MacKenzie, were the most popular political figures of the century; but then MacKenzie, as Solicitor General of the United States, found the tentacles of the Equity Trust reached even into Greg Tolland's office; and MacKenzie was both implacable and incorruptible. The result was more loss of confidence, more disgust with democracy, more disillusionment among voters who now believed that the citizens could never control their government.

While the United States was paralyzed by scandals, and the Soviet Union was rocked by nationalistic movements within its empire, a few international corporations banded together to create the first industrial satellites and the first laser-launching system. The heiress Laurie Jo Hansen built the *Heimdall* industrial satellite and that proved so profitable that other companies first joined with Hansen Enterprises, then set up competing space industries. Based in Zurich and Singapore and Hong Kong and other places of refuge from taxation, the international corporations moved into space even as governments found themselves unable to do so.

Governments looked with envy on the high profits and great potential of space industries. Tolland's lieutenant, Aeneas MacKenzie, led the fight for US takeover of the Hansen empire, ensnarling Hansen Enterprises in a web of legal problems, taxes, regulations, complexities; he might have ended with Hansen nationalized by the United States had not he found corruption in Tolland's staff, and been forced from his office by the President he had created. MacKenzie had to flee for his life; and he had no place to go but to his enemies. From Tolland's Washington MacKenzie went to Laurie Jo Hansen; and because he had known Laurie Jo many years before, and because she with the whole world knew that Aeneas MacKenzie's pledged word was worth more than his life, he became first her consort, then her prime minister, finally her partner.

Yet Tolland and the People's Alliance never forgot who had ruined Tolland's dreams of a country remade by whatever means he thought were needed; his agents had been relentless in pursuit, until Laurie Jo sold out most of her empire to found Diana Station, and took her minister-consort to the Moon: Not even the President of the United States could follow them there.

* * *

And by now no one is interested in killing us, Aeneas thought. Except Greg, and he has no real power. The People's Alliance protected him from the scandals, but the real leadership doesn't trust him. Not any more.

The office door opened without warning and he swiveled quickly. After more than twenty years he loved the sight of her. The red hair was dyed now, he suspected, but he had never asked and never would; and despite all the temptations of low gravity, she had kept her figure. Her smile lit the office.

"She's safe," Laurie Jo said.

"For a while."

"Can't you ever simply be happy without worrying about the future?" She did not wait for an answer. Instead she crossed the office quickly and sat in his lap. They kissed with the affection that comes only from long friendship and love. Then Aeneas opened a desk drawer, took out papers from the computer printer concealed there and began to read.

Although she desperately wanted to know what the message said, she did not read over his shoulder, but waited until he had finished the first sheet. He handed it to her without looking up and read the next. There were only two. Then he waited until she had finished.

"They're on Ceres," Laurie Jo said. "With the cargo safe."

"And someone tried to kill her. At least twice. Someone knows," Aeneas said. He cursed, softly. "I'm a fool. I underestimated the danger."

"She knew the risks," Laurie Jo said. "And who else could we trust with something this important?"

"It was a stupid plan. I should never have let her go."

Laurie Jo laughed. "Could you have stopped her?" she demanded. "No one could control *us* at her age, and she believes in this. You could not have stopped me when I was her age."

"God knows I couldn't."

It had been so long ago. She'd been Laurie Jo Preston then, an orphan girl living alone under the guardianship of bankers and supported by trust funds. They'd met at UCLA when Aeneas was political manager for Greg Tolland. No one had ever heard of Greg Tolland then. The young Congressman, just beginning his meteoric career, was one of the founders of the tiny movement that would one day be the People's Alliance, but then it was nothing more than a dream shared by Tolland and Aeneas.

Aeneas and Laurie Jo Preston had two years. They lived together and hitchhiked across the nation, through Mexico and Baja. They sang and drank and made love and were happy with their dreams until her bankers came to tell her that her name was Hansen, not Preston, and that she had inherited one of the largest fortunes on Earth; then everything changed. "I couldn't control you, and I almost lost you forever," Aeneas said.

"Hush." She put a finger gently on his lips, then bent to kiss him again.

"I miss her," Aeneas said.

"I have missed her terribly from the day she decided to go to Earth," Laurie Jo said. "But I'm proud of her."

"And so am I. Laurie Jo, I feel so helpless! Someone knows. If they tried to kill her once, they'll try again. Before she even left Earth! And she didn't tell us."

"Because we would have stopped her."

"It doesn't make sense," Aeneas said. "They tried to kill her before she ever got to the ship. And they tried to stop the ship from landing on Ceres. That makes no sense at all! We hadn't expected trouble before she got to Ceres. They need that cargo as much as we do—"

"My darling husband," Laurie Jo said. "Use your brains. You're letting this be too personal—"

"How could it be otherwise?"

"—and you're making mistakes because of that. Someone wants to stop the ship from landing. They tried. Perhaps it was Pacifico—have you asked for his dossier?"

"Presently. Not yet."

"More likely someone else," Laurie Jo said. "But whoever it was didn't want *Wayfarer* to land at all. We hadn't expected that."

"No." Aeneas leaned back in his high-backed chair and pressed the tips of his fingers together. His eyes half closed, and his hands pressed gently together, drew apart, pressed together again.

Laurie Jo smiled as she watched him. This was more to her liking. This was the man who had brought down a President.

"So there's another group working in the Belt," Aeneas said.

"You don't sound surprised."

"With billions at stake, I would not be surprised if everyone in the Belt were corrupt," Aeneas said. "How many can resist that kind of temptation? When it is quite feasible to offer bribes in the millions and still make fabulous profits? I expect this was done by the Africans. They don't fancy competition from asteroid mines."

"I don't much blame them," Laurie Jo said. There was sadness in her voice. "They don't have anything to sell except their minerals, and we're driving the price down and down."

Aeneas nodded. They'd discussed all this before. Ruin for the African bloc meant prosperity for the rest of the world; cheap iron and steel and copper and aluminum, the basic stuff of industrial civilization, would let billions live well who now had no hope at all. Eventually it would mean prosperity for the Africans themselves, but not soon, and not for those who now controlled the African bloc.

"So we are facing two sets of enemies," Laurie Jo said.

"Probably more. At least two. One group wishes

to stop the shipments altogether. I doubt they have finished. They'll keep trying, but they won't have many allies in the Belt. It's the others I worry about —and George Lange is dead. She won't have his help." Aeneas leaned back again, his hands moving slowly and gently.

Laurie Jo waited. "VALKYRIE STATUS REPORT." The words formed in her head with no accent, but she always knew when she heard Aeneas speak to the computer, although she could not have told how that was different from hearing the computer report to her.

"READY FOR DEPARTURE IN FIVE HUNDRED HOURS," the computer told them.

"EARLIEST POSSIBLE ARRIVAL TIME ON CERES?"

"ONE HUNDRED AND TWENTY DAYS FROM PRESENT TIME."

"With Lange dead, we'll have to send someone else," Aeneas said.

"Who? There's no one we can trust with something this important. And neither of us can go. Nothing has changed, Aeneas. We're needed here. If we lose control now, there's no point to any of this. We'll lose everything we've worked hard for."

"I know. We can only trust ourselves. Or the boy. Or we could give it all up."

"Neither of us will."

"No. Neither of us will."

She didn't care for the tone he had used, and she looked at him sternly. He was leaning back again, his fingers moving in the familiar pattern that she knew meant he was lost in thought; and she was frightened even before he spoke again.

"There's a better way," he said. "The boy's more valuable here."

"*No*." Her voice rose. "I lost you for sixteen years once! And then almost lost you again, when we'd just found each other. I will not be separated from you again. I will not."

"Laurie Jo." His voice was very calm now. "You can manage the finances. You're better at it than I am, and you *must* stay here; but I've outgrown my usefulness."

"That's not true, you're the base commander—"

"A function that Kit Penrose can fill as well as I can," Aeneas said. "And Kit can train young Aeneas, who will be far more useful here than floundering around out in the Belt. He's not ready for this, Laurie Jo. I don't think our daughter was ready either, but I know our son isn't. He can help you, yes. He understands boardroom tactics, and he's becoming a better engineer than Kit, but he does not know intrigue and corruption. Not yet."

"Nor do you!" she shouted.

"Now really, Laurie Jo—"

"Aeneas, it has been twenty years since you were Solicitor General—"

"Laurie Jo." His voice was quiet and his tone calm.

"And I won't lose you again—"

"I am still a very careful man," Aeneas said. "There is not much risk to me—and I am less valuable than our son. We cannot risk both heirs. If it is a choice between myself and young Aeneas, there is no choice at all, nor would I be—" He stopped, because her face had changed.

She had lost her anger. Now her expression held only sadness.

"You know I'm right," he said. He was not insisting; he merely stated a fact they both understood. She nodded; then buried her face against his shoulder.

"I love you," she said. Then she tried once more, but only because she had to: "Couldn't Kit go? Or—"

"He couldn't, and there is no one else. Not for this. Is there?"

"No. You or our son."

"And thus me." He kissed her gently. "We have twenty days. And when I return, we'll have many more. I'll come back, Laurie Jo. I always have."

"Yes," she said, and she turned away from him quickly so that he would not see the glistening tears in her blue eyes.

XIII

Henri Stoire was a satisfied man, and what's more, he was certain he had every right to be pleased with himself. Since he'd come to Ceres as Interplanet's resident general manager, the output of the mines and refineries had tripled. The enormous mylar plastic mirror, over two kilometers in diameter, hung in synchronous orbit 760 kilometers above the asteroid, providing heat and light for the colony twenty-four hours a day (he still thought of days as having twenty-four hours even though Ceres rotates once each nine hours, five minutes). More miners arrived each month, the capacity of the refineries continued to expand, and a prospecting party had found a large vein of nearly pure water-ice deep under the surface, thus insuring both drinking water and reaction fuel for the nuclear ships like *Wayfarer*.

Henri Stoire was satisfied, but his superiors were not. His production goals were set in Zurich by men who knew nothing of the conditions on Ceres, but who knew a lot about international competition, manipulation of commodity futures, and always about banking and money; the goals they set were high. Of course, Henri thought, when he tried to be fair—not very often—the costs of the Ceres operation were very high as well. It took eleven new francs to get one kilogram from Earth's surface to Earth orbit, a hundred more to get it to Ceres, and Ceres required thousands of metric tonnes of supplies, food, equipment, and men, always more men. The return had to be high or the investment couldn't be justified.

Henri met their ever-increasing production goals, but his costs were always higher than estimated. No incentive bonuses for Stoire, not this year. Perhaps when a full cargo from the Belt reached Earth orbit . . . even iron ore delivered to Earth orbit would be highly valuable for more orbital factory construction. Iron in orbit would sell for almost Fr. 12,000 a metric tonne, and Henri had ten thousand tonnes to ship, along with one thousand tonnes of tin (Fr. 6,720,000), fifteen hundred tonnes of nearly pure silver (Fr. 315,000,000) and a few hundred million francs' worth of assorted other metals. The total value of the cargo he would shortly send down would be considerably more than half a billion francs; a respectable sum indeed. Now he had only to get the shipment to Earth. The incentive bonuses would follow.

Actually, Interplanet's bonuses interested Henri far less than his employers—or at least most of them—knew. True, Henri had enormous debts, the result of unwise speculations: had he known as much about the international commodity market as the men who set his production goals did, Henri would never have come to Ceres in the first place. His debts were further increased by Henri's unfortunate addiction to chemin-de-fer and roulette, and his even less fortunate tendency to borrow money from any source available. He had been born a rich man, of a great and wealthy family, and he had lost everything; he needed money.

Although Zurich's bonuses were not small by normal standards, Henri needed far more money than could be acquired by ordinary means. Had his employers known just how much money Henri owed, they would never have sent him to Ceres, or anywhere else; but his creditors were careful men who never advertised the names of those who borrowed from them; and they had many suggestions for Henri. There was no way, bonuses or not, that Henri could earn what he owed; but with any luck he would leave Ceres with his debts paid and more money than he had ever had in his life. If all that was merely a small part of the profits his creditors would make from his work, Henri was not an avaricious man. He truly believed that he asked for no more than he was entitled to and certainly he had high abilities.

Henri was a small man, very neat in appearance. Even on Ceres he looked neat, and that was often very difficult. His small size was no handicap in space. In many ways it was a decided advantage. In low gravity long legs were mostly good for running into hard objects and otherwise getting in the way.

Though small, Henri was no weakling. He exercised daily and he was always willing to give the men a hand with a tough job. Henri could do the job of nearly any man in his employ; he took great pride in that, and it was certainly a useful ability.

Some of his latest activities, those in favor of his creditors and unknown to his employers in Zurich, could not have been accomplished if Henri had not understood every detail of the automated refinery operation, known how to construct conveyor systems, dig out chambers in rock with explosives. . . .

Those skills, though needed, were not the key to his plan for resuming his place among the idle rich in Monte Carlo. More important than any of them was the study he had made of computer operations. That was the key to it all, and it had gone so smoothly that had Henri been a superstitious man, he might have been frightened.

Sometimes he was appalled by what he was doing. He felt no guilt about betraying the Directors of the Interplanet combine; if they paid him what he was worth, he would not have to resort to embezzlement (Henri preferred to think of it as misallocation of company resources, or even as a legitimate perquisite to his office). He felt no guilt, but he was sometimes disturbed by the sheer magnitude of the operation. Not only was something like one hundred million francs involved—and that was a large enough sum to impress even Henri Stoire—but also the follow-up implications would be even larger. Mankind had never succeeded in getting nuclear fusion to work on a commercial scale. Fission worked fine and had since the 1950's, but the far more valuable and efficient fusion process continued to be too expensive, too difficult; and the result was a continuing energy crisis that affected nearly every nation on Earth. Fertilizer prices depended on energy prices, which meant that energy prices controlled how much the poor would eat. Cheap fusion would bring cheap food—and Henri was turning fusion over to a gang of international criminals.

Still, he felt no guilt. If food was dear, it was because people were cheap. If the fools wished their children to eat well, let them either work to earn enough money or have fewer children. It was no concern of Henri's what happened to children in India, Bangla-Desh, Africa, South America. . . .

Nor was he worried about being caught. As manager for Interplanet he controlled the only police force on Ceres. The company guards worked for him and took his orders. The accountants reported to him and could only gain access to the computer through him. They could ask Interplanet's computer questions as long as they liked; even if they knew the real questions they should ask, it would not tell them without his authorization, and they didn't know anyway. Besides, in a few weeks it would all be over, and there would be no record of what Henri had done.

Henri Stoire sat at his desk, the only real desk on Ceres and a mark of his importance, and despite his satisfaction with himself and his work, he frowned as he read the report brought to him by Captain Greiner.

Wayfarer had arrived with cargo intact; excellent. But someone had tried to prevent the ship from coming to Ceres, and that was not. *Wayfarer*'s cargo was the key to everything. Without it they would never get all that iron and copper and tin and silver to Earth. Who had done this?

It took him only moments to dismiss Pacifico. The lawyer had been sent by Zurich, and was rumored to be a clever accountant as well. He would have been a nuisance, and it was as well that he was dead; but he had almost certainly not been responsible for nearly crippling *Wayfarer*. No. It was very likely that Pacifico's part was exactly what he had said it was, a frightened man trying to keep Captain Greiner from taking high risks with the ship.

Nor was it likely that the missing George Lange had been the saboteur. The Daedalus Corporation had far too much at stake, and they hired carefully. Daedalus was responsible for getting Henri's cargo safely back to Earth; the loss of one of their senior engineers would be inconvenient, possibly worse than that. All true. But Daedalus had a deeper role in this game. Henri's creditors had warned him that Daedalus, supposedly owned by other Zurich bankers and itself one of the stockholders in the consortium that created Interplanet, had its nose in far too many places. His creditors suspected that Daedalus worked for very powerful interests indeed—possibly even for MacKenzie and Hansen; that Daedalus engineers were often spies reporting to Interplanet stockholders, and whenever they were around, Henri should be careful. The warning was appreciated but not needed; Henri was always careful. But it made it unlikely that Lange had tried to sabotage *Wayfarer*. Far more probably Lange had been snooping around and had caught the saboteur, and was put outside the ship for his trouble.

So who might it be? Henri scanned the passenger

and crew lists. Anyone might be an African sympathizer—Henri had already concluded the African bloc was the most likely sponsor of the sabotage—and that would not necessarily show in the kind of resumes sent out with passengers. Or the saboteur could be working for money. He lifted a microphone.

"READY," the computer said.

"I WANT COMPLETE DOSSIERS ON ALL PASSENGERS AND CREW ARRIVING ABOARD WAYFARER. HIGHEST PRIORITY REQUEST TO ZURICH HEADQUARTERS. JUSTIFICATION: NECESSITY TO IDENTIFY SABOTEUR."

"ACKNOWLEDGED."

He returned to his scrutiny of the passenger list. He read names and specialties, paying no particular attention to what he saw, until he came to "Norsedal, Jacob. Computer Specialist. To be supervisor of computer operations, Interplanet."

He read it again, then cursed. Zurich had not told him of this! True, he had requested a new programmer, but he was satisfied with his computer staff and its acting head. He had certainly not sent for any experts to take control; under his present arrangement Henri himself was the real supervisor of computer operations, and he liked it that way.

This could be bothersome, especially now. Did Zurich suspect something? He would have to be very careful with this Norsedal. Was Norsedal curious? An agent of Zurich? He must be watched closely. Henri continued to scan the list.

MacMillan, Ellen. Engineer, no employer. Henri smiled at that. Every ship brought two or three unemployed single women, and most claimed to be some kind of engineer. They might very well have their degrees, but generally they made a great deal more money in a far older occupation. He wondered where the MacMillan girl would go: to one of the established houses, or would she prey on the miners and prospectors and refinery workers from her own quarters? From curiosity he lifted the microphone again. "I WANT A PHOTOGRAPH OF ELLEN MACMILLAN, PASSENGER ON WAYFARER."

"ACKNOWLEDGED."

A few seconds later the facsimile emerged from a slot at the side of his desk. He looked it over, smiling at the blonde hair and blue eyes, pug nose; a pretty girl, young, one who would command a high price, for a while. Then the smile faded. Was there something familiar about the face? Where might he have seen it before?

No. He was certain he had never seen the girl. But she reminded him of someone. He did not know who, but it was disturbing. She reminded him of someone he feared. He laughed to himself, because he feared no one; but he kept the photograph and put a tick mark against her name on the list to remind him to take some care with her dossier when it arrived.

Henri Stoire was a careful man indeed.

XIV

Kevin wandered through rock corridors, not quite lost but not entirely sure of where he was. He was somewhere inside the Ceres complex and as long as he did not go through an airtight door, he couldn't be very far from the central area; but he was looking for Ellen and he didn't have any idea of where to find her.

When *Wayfarer* landed, the passengers had to help unload the ship and transfer cargo—most of the cargo, Kevin reminded himself. One compartment remained sealed. When Kevin's share of the work was over, many of the passengers had already gone inside. Kevin followed through the airlock doors, relieved to be off the harsh and barren surface of the asteroid. No one would say that Ceres was a pretty place, although the stars were spectacular; but Kevin had had enough stars to last him a long time.

Why had Ellen left without telling him where she was going? he wondered. He would have to report in for work soon, and they might not have much time together until he could find out where he would be stationed. Then they could arrange something more permanent.

The corridors shone. They had been painted with plastic to seal in air leaks, so that it was possible to move around inside the Ceres Station without a helmet. There were lights at intervals. Kevin hoped to see someone to ask directions from, but before he did, he came to a signpost.

It showed DAEDALUS CORPORATE OFFICES just one corridor down. Kevin went there eagerly. They could tell him where he would be staying.

There was an elderly man in the Daedalus Corporation offices. The offices themselves were merely two rooms cut in raw rock off the corridor. They were obviously little used; there was almost no furniture, and an automatic message-recording system was the only piece of large office equipment.

The man was well over fifty, with a network of red lines around his mouth and chin that betrayed long exposure to face masks. He had wrinkles at the corners of his eyes, and much gray in his hair. He frowned at Kevin. "You'll be Senecal."

"Yes."

"I'm John Eliot. Senior man for Daedalus out here. You got our other people with you?"

"No—"

"You should have. You're an engineer. It's your responsibility to look after non-professional employees. Now we'll have to go find them. We don't have much time. Time, Senecal, is the most valuable commodity in the Belt just now."

"Yes, sir. Look, Mr. Eliot—"

"Call me Johnny. We'll either be friends or you'll hate me before long, but either way, it works better if we use first names."

"Johnny. Yes, sir. I am Kevin."

"Yeah. I know. You were saying something?"

"Mr.—Johnny, this is my first job. I'm no professional. I'm just an engineering student, and the idea of my looking after people twice my age is funny. They wouldn't take orders from me."

"We'll see. Did they get on all right with Lange?"

"Yes, sir."

"Too bad about him," Eliot said. "What happened, anyway?"

Kevin explained all he knew. "George just vanished," he finished. "Never did find him, no trace of him. Nothing."

"His stuff missing?"

"No," Kevin said. "Captain Greiner has it. He didn't know what to do with it."

"We'll collect it before we go up. May as well see to that, and to finding our workmen. You can leave that gear here."

"All right." Kevin set down the travel cases he carried and started to go out into the corridor.

"Nope," Eliot said. "Get your hat. Didn't they teach you that? First rule, never go *anywhere* without your helmet. We don't often have blowouts on Ceres, but it only takes one to kill you if you don't have your hat with you. Remember that."

"Yes, sir." Kevin retrieved his helmet, then thoughtfully put on his tool belt as well.

"Good," Eliot said. "Now let's go." He led the way through the bare rock corridor. "They'll probably be at Fat Jack's," Eliot said. "Most head there when they get off work or off a ship. Surprised you didn't get there first."

"I was hoping someone would tell me where I will be staying," Kevin said. "I didn't see any hotels—"

Eliot laughed. "Hell, you won't be staying on Ceres."

"Sir? Johnny? If we won't be staying on Ceres, where will we be?"

"Didn't Lange tell you anything?" Eliot demanded. "Don't you even know what you'll be working on?"

"No, sir. I asked once, and he said I'd find out in due time. But I never did."

Eliot laughed. "Well, that was the company's orders all right, but it's damn foolishness. Everybody on Ceres knows our big secret, not that it's anything to be secret about anyway. Daedalus is responsible for the delivery system to get cargo to Earth. We're building it. I expect Lange kept everything about that a big secret too?"

"Yes—"

"Okay. Up there about a thousand kilometers above Ceres there's a rock a couple of hundred meters in diameter. It's mostly nickel-iron, good stuff. We're busily mining out corridors and putting in life-support systems. When we're done, we'll pack it with all the refined minerals Interplanet has collected and take it home."

"Take a two-hundred-meter rock home? How?" Kevin demanded. "It must weigh five million tonnes—"

"Thirty million," Eliot said. "Hell, it's simple.

We put hydrogen bombs at just the right place—
have to calculate the center of gravity pretty
carefully—and light 'em off. Do that a few times
and we'll have that rock in just the right transfer
orbit. Off she goes to Earth. Down there they do it
again to stop it. No sweat." Eliot chuckled. He was
obviously enjoying the look on Kevin's face.
"Lange really didn't tell you, eh? Well, that's what
we're up to. You brought the bombs with you, on
Wayfarer. That's why everybody got so excited
down here when we heard you were in trouble.
Needed the H-bombs. Without 'em, we'd really
have troubles. No other way to get all that stuff
home."

"And somebody's going to ride this thing to
Earth?" Kevin said.

"Sure. Safest place around. There'll be a couple
of hundred meters of nickel-iron and rock between
the crew and the bombs—what could happen?"

That made sense, but Kevin still didn't like the
idea much. "Are we supposed to be the crew?"

"Naw. Interplanet provides the crew. They
wouldn't trust a half-billion francs' worth of cargo
to anybody but their own people. Understand the
manager, Mr. Stoire himself, is going. Guess I
can't blame them much."

They moved on through the rock corridor. In
Ceres's low gravity they couldn't walk, nor could
they simply glide from place to place as they would
in no gravity at all. Instead they moved in a series
of bounds, like oversized kangaroos.

They came to a cross corridor, and Eliot turned
down it. There were bright lights at the end, their

glare contrasting with the dim light in the corridor. They heard sounds: shouting and singing. Happy sounds.

"That's Fat Jack's place," Eliot said. "Best bar on Ceres. Mainly because it's the only bar here. Pretty good place, though. You can get nearly anything you want. Not that you'll be here all that often."

Kevin had already thought of that. "Don't we get to come—down to Ceres?"

"Sure, the company provides recreation trips when we're caught up on the work. Don't cost that much to run the scooters."

It looked as if everyone who had come in *Wayfarer,* and half the permanent crew of Ceres, were packed into Fat Jack's. The proprietor was a burly man with no legs. When one of the newcomers asked why he hadn't gone back to Earth, the owner laughed.

"Sure, they'll pay my way back and give me a goddam pension, but I don't want it. What the hell use is a cripple on Earth? Out here I don't need legs." He waved to indicate the crowd in his saloon. "I make my own beer and whiskey and I get good prices. I've got a thousand friends. What do I want with Earth?"

The saloon consisted of a large chamber carved from rock, a few tables and booths, and one long bar running across the back of the room.

All the drinks were served in covered containers with straws, although most of the customers had learned the art of popping open the top, sucking out a drink, and closing it before their beer or whiskey drifted away.

Kevin pointed out the Daedalus employees, and Eliot went to round them up. While Kevin was waiting, Ellen came in. Bill Dykes was with her.

"Hi," Kevin shouted. He went over to them. "Glad I found you. They want me to go up to one of Ceres's moons—"

"C-4," Dykes said. "The one they're fitting up as a spaceship."

"Right. How did you know?" Kevin asked.

Dykes shrugged. "No secret what Daedalus does. Everybody on Ceres knows about the H-bombs. Wonder why they were so damn close-mouthed aboard *Wayfarer*?"

"Well, they *are* hydrogen bombs," Kevin said.

"Sure. And bombs can kill people. Lots of other ways to get killed out here. I need a drink. You, Ellie?"

"Yes, thank you."

Dykes went to fight his way to the bar.

"I get some recreation visits," Kevin said. "I won't see you often at first, only when I'm down. Where will you be staying?"

"I—I'll be staying with Bill," Ellen said.

It took Kevin a moment to understand what she had said. "In his—"

"Yes, I'll be living with him."

"But—damn it, he's old enough to be your father!" Kevin shouted. He wanted to say more: That at first she had put him off because she didn't want lasting attachments, and now they were lovers, and what was this? Bitterness made him say more: "I get it. He can pay you more than I can."

"It's none of your damned business," she said. She spoke loudly, so that many of the people in the

163

bar could hear her. "You don't own me and you have no right to make judgments."

"No. I don't suppose I do," Kevin said. "Except —except that I thought we were friends."

"If you're my friend, you don't act much like it," Ellen said.

"Trouble, Ellie?" Dykes was back, without the drinks he'd gone after.

"Not really," she said.

"Kevin. Are you about ready to leave?" John Eliot called.

"Yes. I'll wait for you outside," Kevin said. He turned and left without looking at Ellen.

"Hell, this place is getting to be a drag," Bill Dykes said. His voice carried through the room and out to where Kevin stood. "Let's split and throw our own party."

"All right," Ellen giggled. It was obvious what kind of party Dykes had in mind. She followed the miner out. They came past Kevin, and as they did, Ellen said, very quietly, "Kevin. Please. I know you don't understand, but please trust me. And for God's sake, don't let anyone know I've said anything to you. Make people believe you hate me." With that she went on without looking back, and when Dykes made a loud ribald comment about Kevin, she laughed.

* * *

Ceres has five moons, if you can call small rocks a few hundred meters in diameter "moons." Three of them had been extensively mined, but two had been temporarily abandoned when better grades of ore were found on Ceres itself. The other one, C-4, was Kevin's home for the next few weeks.

There was plenty of work and not enough people to do it. First, the asteroid had to be surveyed to find the exact center of gravity. Once that was located, a pit was to be dug for the hydrogen bombs that would be used to turn the tiny moon into an enormous rocket ship. On the opposite side the Daedalus crew would carve out chambers for the crew to live in, more compartments for the gold and silver and copper and other refined metals produced on Ceres. Meanwhile, another crew would set up huge mirrors on C-4 and use those to concentrate sunlight so they could boil and refine the ores extracted from the planetoid. "No point in wasting anything," Eliot had said.

When they were finished, C-4 would carry a cargo worth half a billion francs. In addition, the asteroid itself would be valuable—nearly ten million metric tonnes of nickel-iron which would end up in Earth orbit. Refineries there would extract the iron to use in space construction. Even the twenty million tonnes of rock would be useful in orbit. The asteroid could be used as a platform.

Kevin's job was installation of the life-support equipment for the flight crew. With the help of miners and a lot of mining machinery, he hollowed out the crew chambers, then sprayed them with a thick coating of plastic; when the plastic dried, the chambers were airtight. Air lock doors were machined from chunks of the moonlet itself, and set on hinges. Sometimes the whole structure reminded Kevin more of a series of bank vaults than a spaceship; everything was massive, and rather crudely made.

There were no work shifts, there was simply a

job that had to be done. Eliot explained what was needed and was available for consultation. Otherwise he left Kevin alone. When one task was completed Eliot would check it out, then assign another.

Kevin found the job exacting, but it was important work, and everyone was enthusiastic about it. They were taking part in something that might change man's future.

"Think about it," Eliot said. "If we can get all of Earth's metals out here, they won't have to strip-mine on Earth. No pollution down there. You know, in fifty years Earth can be one big park, with all the industries out in space."

Kevin became lost in a maze of calculations: food, oxygen, and water consumption for a crew of two (with standby provision for three) on a trip four hundred days long; g stresses which the equipment would endure when the one-megaton H-bombs went off; finding stress seams in the nickel-iron moonlet so they could be reinforced. Slowly the "ship" began to look like something that could support human life, with fuel cells for electric power, caves of ice for water and cooling, telescopes and radar for finding the exact position; navigation computer, galley, bunk rooms—with a separate stateroom for each of the crew, there being no space limits at all.

Finally Eliot relented and took the work crew down to Ceres. They went in a scooter much like the one used to get from the Earth satellite to *Wayfarer:* an open framework with seats for the passengers, a baggage compartment, and a large kerosene-oxygen rocket engine. The scooters also had a navigation computer; C-4 moved around Ceres at more than a third of a kilometer each second, and the total velocity change needed to get from the "moon" to Ceres was more than eight hundred miles an hour. The transfer orbit was tricky.

Kevin talked with the scooter pilot in Fat Jack's after they arrived on Ceres.

"Yeah, sure, I could eyeball it," Hal Donnelly said. "But it'd be tough. Not like flying an airplane." Donnelly had once been a test pilot, and would be one of the crew accompanying C-4 on the long trip to Earth. "Airplanes have air to work with. You can turn a corner, or slow down. Scooter doesn't work that way."

Kevin wasn't really listening to the pilot. He was thinking about Ellen. There had been so much work on C-4 that he hadn't had much time to brood about her before—except when he was ready to go to sleep at night—but he had felt a quick excitement when Eliot announced they were going down to Ceres, and he hoped to see her. He didn't know what to say to her, but there had to be some way—

He didn't know how to ask about her. He was afraid of what he would hear. His fellow workers on C-4 had talked about the various prostitutes on Ceres, and although none of them had mentioned Ellen by name, they all assumed that any single woman who came out not under contract to one of the companies could have only one purpose in mind.

Why the hell was she living with Bill Dykes? She'd hardly spoken to Dykes on the ship. She certainly hadn't known him very well, yet she moved in with him her first day on Ceres. It didn't make sense.

Of course it makes sense, Kevin thought. She likes the guy and I just didn't know it. She's got every right to move in with anybody she wants to and you've got no call to be jealous about it. She said everything would be over when they got to Ceres. It was just a shipboard thing. He could tell himself that, but it didn't help.

"You haven't heard a damned thing I said," Hal Donnelly said. "You drink my liquor but you don't listen to me." The pilot was grinning slightly.

"Oh—uh, sorry," Kevin said.

"No sweat. I know what you need. I'm about to go looking for a little poon myself. I know a good house. Want to come along?"

The idea was not attractive. Kevin still hoped to meet Ellen. He knew that wasn't very reasonable, and that she was likely to be with someone else, but there was always a chance—"Thanks, Hal. Not just yet. I'll have a couple more."

The pilot shrugged. "Suit yourself. We lift out of here in thirty-four hours. Meet you here."

"Right. And thanks for the drink."

" 'S okay. You'll get me one next time. Right now I've got a more urgent urge. . . ." Hal grinned again and left the bar.

And just what the hell am I doing here? Kevin wondered. I don't know anybody in this place. He ordered another drink. The vacuum-distilled whiskey was rough and strong and cost too much. Kevin sipped at it disconsolately.

He didn't want to leave because Fat Jack's was the place where everyone came to find people. The recreation schedule for the C-4 crew was known and posted in Fat Jack's: If Ellen wanted to see him, she'd know where to find him.

Jacob Norsedal came into the bar. "Hello," he said. He took a place across from Kevin. There was no real need to sit in Ceres' low gravity, but the habit dies hard; and it is convenient to anchor yourself in one place. "I've been computing the trajectory your moonlet will take back to Earth."

"I'm still not sure this will work," Kevin said.

Norsedal looked surprised. "Of course it will. Think of it as a fusion spacedrive. Plenty of energy in a megaton. One million tons of TNT, ten-to-the-twenty-second ergs. . . ."

"I wasn't thinking about the energy," Kevin said. "It's the navigation. We can't really locate the center of gravity all that well—too much guesswork."

"Run it off," Norsedal said. He offered his belt computer. "Takes a lot of energy to get that much iron to rotate. So they're off a little—you've got little tamped-implosion kiloton bombs to correct that, and the rocket motors for fine adjustment."

"Yeah, I've seen the numbers," Kevin said. "It looks silly as hell, mounting big rocket engines on the ground. Big things." The four Saturn-sized rocket engines were mounted in a cruciform pattern, pointing away from the center of the cross. They would be used to turn C-4 in the right direction. "But it's still using *bombs*." Kevin said.

Norsedal shrugged. It was obvious that to him bombs were just another device to channel energy; it was doubtful that he thought of them as bombs at all, or even imagined the real devices. They were more input numbers into his equations, data to be fed into the computer. "Have you seen much of Ceres?" Jacob asked.

"No. I was only here a few hours after *Wayfarer* landed, and this is my first trip down since."

"Well, I know a good place to eat," Norsedal said. "The food in the Interplanet commissary is all right, but it's nothing to rave about. I can find some real steaks—"

"Steaks! Terrific. We've been eating reconstituted stew. And textured vegetable proteins. And—"

"Spare me those horrors," Norsedal said. He patted his ample belly. "If I had to eat that way, I'd waste to nothing. Come on, let's get a good dinner." He hustled Kevin out of the bar and off to one of the rock corridors.

Ceres was honeycombed with passages. Some were still used as working mines. Others were abandoned mine shafts, now used as part of the living quarters. There were airlocks at intervals along the corridors.

Jacob led the way through a maze of passages, and soon they were a long way from the inhabited parts of Ceres Station.

"Where the hell are we going?" Kevin demanded.

"Short cut." Norsedal continued to scurry

along. As he'd predicted when Kevin first met him, his weight and ungainly appearance were no handicaps in low gravity. They turned another corner and went upward. There was an airlock there.

Jacob came very close to Kevin and spoke softly, almost a whisper. "We're going outside now. Please, just follow me, and don't use your suit radio whatever you do."

"But—why?" Kevin kept his voice low to match Norsedal's.

"Will you trust me? It's important."

Kevin nodded. He'd known Norsedal through the whole trip out; whatever Jacob was doing, it wasn't dishonest. He put on his helmet.

Norsedal opened the airlock and they went through the double doors. It was night outside on Ceres, but the overhead synchronous satellite mirror left the surface bathed in light. Down in the crevasse where the airlock opened they could see only by starlight, and Norsedal did not use a flash. He led the way, Kevin following closely.

Then he turned into a cavern so deep that there was no light at all. He went on, downward, and turned a corner before he switched on a flash. Then he gestured, finger to lips, and went around another turn.

There was an inflatable shelter there with its own airlock. The outer door stood open. Jacob gestured toward it, then followed Kevin in. There was the hiss of pumps and the airlock chamber pressurized, then the inner door opened.

Ellen MacMillan was inside.

XV

"I don't think anyone noticed us leaving," Norsedal said. "But I'll have to get back quickly. I have to go on duty in the computer center."

Kevin hardly heard him. He was staring at Ellen. He thought she was lovely. "But—"

"We'll explain," she said. "I wanted to keep you out of this, Kevin, but I can't. I need help. Will you help me?"

"I'll try. But—"

"Yes. It's such a long story, I don't know where to begin," she said. "Kevin, I didn't come here to work as an engineer. Or to be a prostitute, either."

"I never thought that," Kevin said quickly.

"That's sweet of you. But I hope everybody else does," she said. "I'm really not very good at the secret-agent business. Kevin, I—I work for some of the owners of Interplanet. For Hansen Enterprises. They have a contract for all the Arthurium mined in the Belt."

Arthurium. One of the super-heavy elements. In the first quarter of the Twentieth Century scientists thought there were only ninety-two elements. Then the nuclear engineers discovered they could make plutonium, and californium, and a host of other elements heavier than uranium-92, but all the new elements were unstable. Finally a stable natural element, atomic number of 124, was discovered. In the years that followed other super-heavy elements were found, but only in trace amounts. The super-heavies were in the cores of the planets, and planetary cores are hard to get to: thousands of miles underground.

Ceres was only a couple of hundred miles in radius, but had once been the core of a much larger planet: there were super-heavy elements in abundance. Abundance is a relative term, of course: The supers are still very rare, found only in fractions-of-a-percent concentration; but they were available, and the most valuable of all was Arthurium, a member of the Tin-Niobium family, with the property of being superconductive at temperatures far higher than any other known super-conductors.

"And somebody is stealing the Arthurium," Jacob Norsedal said. "I'm sure of it."

"That's what I came out to look into," Ellen said. "When the manager here reported only a few kilograms of Arthurium had been extracted, we wondered. Understand, it might have been true. Arthurium is very rare. But from the original assay figures, we thought there should be hundreds of kilograms of Arthurium, and we—Hansen Enterprises—needs it. Hansen scientists think they can solve the fusion problem if they have enough!"

Kevin found a place to sit. The shelter wasn't well furnished; in fact it wasn't furnished at all; but there were several boxes of gear stacked at one end next to the pumps and air supply, and Kevin found a perch on them. He tried to digest the information he'd been given. Fusion power would be priceless. And Arthurium, the little that was known to exist, sold for over a hundred thousand francs per kilogram. Hundreds of millions of francs, perhaps billions, were at stake here.

"What do you want with me?" he asked. His voice was harsh.

"Why are you angry?" Ellen asked.

He didn't say anything.

"Dykes," Jacob Norsedal prompted.

"Oh." Ellen smiled. "Kevin, Bill Dykes has known my father for—since long before I was born. He worked for Hansen Enterprises on the Moon. When I needed a place to stay, I had to ask him, because I was afraid someone here might suspect me, and I didn't want anyone else to get hurt. They killed George Lange, don't forget. I have no right to ask your help, but I don't know where else to go."

"You mean—" Kevin's grin was broad and sheepish. "And I almost drove myself crazy thinking about you and—"

"I'm sorry."

"I have to get back," Norsedal said. "If anyone asks, I'll say you didn't want steak after all and went to find a cat house. I doubt that anyone is interested in you, Kevin, but they might be and it's best to have a story."

"I must be stupid," Kevin said. "I don't know where you fit into this, Jacob."

"He's an honest man," Ellen said.

"I was hired by the Zurich office," Norsedal

said. "And I'm supposed to report directly to them if I find anyting wrong. Not that Zurich is suspicious of the management here, but with all that money at stake, they wanted an independent check —to make certain."

"Just as we did," Ellen said. "Only we were suspicious."

"And you found something?" Kevin asked.

"Yes." Norsedal nodded vigorously. "There are whole memory areas in the computer banks that I can't access. And the programs run too long. That means the computer is following instructions that don't appear in the flow diagrams. I haven't found out what's going on yet, but I think I will. I managed to get a print-out of the computer's core, all the instructions. They're in binary of course, so it takes time to analyze what I have, but I'm sure there are operations going on that don't appear in the log. Mining operations, for example."

"And in the refinery," Ellen said. "It wouldn't take much to cover up a few hundred kilograms missing among all the thousands of tons of rock they process, tons of gold they've extracted—"

"And the refinery is nearly automatic," Norsedal added. "I can use the computer to find out just who might be involved by analyzing the work schedules, but I've been afraid to do that until I know just who's been using it and for what. It might be programmed to tell whenever people ask that kind of question." Norsedal went to the airlock and squeezed through the narrow inner door. "Good luck." He closed the lock and started the pumps

"How does he—why are you two working together?" Kevin asked. "Are you sure you can trust him?"

"Yes. Henri Stoire, the manager, sent for dossiers on all the passengers aboard *Wayfarer*. They came twenty hours ago, and Jacob had to pass them along—but he figured out who I am from my resume sheets."

"If he could, so can Stoire—"

"I know," Ellen said. She sounded worried. "That's why I'm here. I don't know what to do. Ever since Stoire got the dossiers, there's been no communication from Ceres to Earth. The equipment has malfunctioned, Stoire says—but Jacob says it hasn't."

"And who are you?" Kevin demanded.

"Do you really want to know—no. Please, Kevin. I don't want to tell you."

"All right." He went to her and held out his arms. After a moment she crossed the tiny distance that remained and kissed him.

"Not very passionate in these pressure suits," Ellen laughed.

"We could—"

She looked at him sharply.

"Oh, hell," he said. "You wanted my help. I won't complicate things by—Ellen, I think I've been in love with you for a long time. Damn it, I know I am. Why else would it have bothered me so much when I thought you were living with Bill Dykes, maybe being—"

She cut him off with another kiss. "We can talk about this later. And we will. We really will. But now—"

"What is it you need?"

"I have to set up communications to reach off Ceres," she said. "Everything happened so fast! I was here for weeks, and I didn't really learn anything. Bill Dykes thought there was something strange happening at the refinery, but he couldn't be sure. They're very careful who they let work there. I didn't really have anything to report, nothing solid to be suspicious about, until Jacob came to tell me about discrepancies he found in the computer log. Now I've got to get a message to the Moon."

"How?" Kevin demanded.

"Bill and Jacob got this equipment," she said. "Bill knew about this shelter, and Jacob was able to cover the communications gear by listing it as lost in the computer inventory. So we have enough electronics and power supply to set up a high-gain antenna and get off our message, only there's too much for me to do by myself. Jacob isn't very good at outside work and he'd be missed if he didn't show up. And Bill thinks they've been watching him ever since he began asking questions. A few hours ago they gave him a special overtime assignment, that's not unusual, and if he didn't take it, they'd know something was wrong—so I couldn't think of anyone to help, and Jacob knew the scooter would be down from C-4 and he went to find you and I hoped you would help me—"

"Shhh. Of course I'll help you." At that moment Kevin would have done anything for her, including digging a hole all the way through to the other side of Ceres. He decided that he liked being in love.

* * *

The gear was heavy. Weight is not a very meaningful concept in gravity as low as Ceres's, but even in low gravity things have mass; large things are hard to start moving, and just as hard to stop. The surface of Ceres is rugged: the asteroid has been battered by collisions with other rocks for billions of years, and there is no atmosphere to smooth out the craters and crags the constant bombardment creates. Carrying several hundred pounds of equipment—even when it only "weighs" thirty pounds or so—is not easy.

Ellen had gotten from Bill Dykes a map of the area around Ceres Station itself, and Dykes had selected a plateau three kilometers away as the best location for the transmitter. It was cut off from the Station by high peaks, but had a good visibility to space. They struggled across the crags and craters with their enormous loads, using their flashlights sparingly, and not talking at all.

Despite the hard work, Kevin felt exuberant, filled with joy and love—and hatred for whomever was trying to thwart the development of fusion power. Kevin remembered the energy shortages in his childhood, and although he knew that what he had called poverty would have been fabulous wealth to much of the world, he could remember the hard times he had grown up in. Fusion could change much of that for the whole world, and it was in danger from selfish people who only wanted money.

They reached the plateau. Kevin came close to Ellen and put his helmet to hers. "We can't get this done without communication," he said.

"Yes. I guess we'll just have to risk using our suit radios at lowest power. I don't think anyone is looking for us. Why would they be?"

"No reason," Kevin said, but he worried anyway. They opened the cases and took out a collapsible antenna. The elements bolted together to form a large aprabolic dish which could be pointed toward Earth.

The work was maddening. Each nut and bolt seemed a live thing, ready to slip from their heavy gloves and fall to vanish in the deep shadows. Connectors and parts which would have been simple to work with inside with plenty of light became complex puzzles, shapes not recognizable from the instruction diagrams.

"Putting together Christmas toys," Ellen said as she searched for a large part that had somehow simply vanished in shadow although it couldn't be more than a meter away.

Eventually they got it done, and began to set up the telescope and quadrant they would use to point the antenna toward Earth's Moon.

"Earth's still below the horizon," Kevin said as they leveled the telescope platform. "I think we're going to make it. Ellen, tell me something."

"Yes?"

"You didn't grow up in any orphanage. They don't assemble Christmas toys in foster homes and orphanages."

"Yes they—"

"And you said the first day I met you that your father—'Daddy' you called him—made you study gymnastics."

"Oh. I'd forgotten I told you that," she said.

"We—I was distracted at the time." She laughed softly.

"So who are you?" Kevin asked.

"Oh come now, Mr. Senecal." The voice was a man's, cultured, and entirely strange to Kevin. Kevin jumped in a startled reaction and almost upset the telescope. "Haven't you guessed that yet? Allow me to introduce you to Miss Glenda Hansen-MacKenzie."

There were two men on the plateau with them. One held a small rifle, the other a pistol. "Please keep your hands where I can see them," the smaller intruder said. "Sorry to interrupt you, but I really don't want you sending messages to Earth. I'm glad we found you in time."

"Who the hell are you?" Kevin demanded.

"It's Henri Stoire," Ellen said.

"Good morning," Stoire said calmly. "Hal, get their tool belts, please."

"Yes, sir."

"Hal Donnelly?" Kevin said.

"Sad but true," the scooter pilot said. "Too bad you had to get mixed up in this, Kevin. And you owe me a drink, too." Donnelly moved expertly, his pistol held well out of reach, and took their tool belts.

"What are you going to do with us?" Ellen demanded.

"Well, now, that is a problem," Stoire said. "There is a great deal of money at stake here. A very great deal. I can hardly allow you to get in my way."

It's happening again, Kevin thought. It was exactly like the time in the alley when the muggers had taken his wallet. He felt violated, humiliated, helpless—and Ellen, no, her name is Glenda he thought irrelevantly, they'll kill her. He tensed, ready to jump at Donnelly. Maybe Glenda could get away if he tried—

"On the other hand, you are worth a great deal of money," Stoire said. "What would your mother and father pay to have you back safe? Our scheme is almost perfect, but we all know there are no perfect plans. Right, Hal?"

"I don't know, sir—"

"There is the sabotage group," Stoire said. "True, I believe I have identified their agent, but suppose I have not? If he were to stop C-4 from going on schedule, we would be left with nothing. It would do no great harm to have Miss Hansen-MacKenzie hidden away, ready to produce when needed. I expect Aeneas MacKenzie would not even be above getting all of us off scot free in exchange for his daughter. It never hurts to have insurance."

"Well, yes sir," Donnelly said. "If you put it that way. But where can we keep them?"

"I believe I have an idea," Stoire said. He moved closer to Donnelly and they spoke helmet to helmet for a moment.

"Right. Come on, let's go," Donnelly said. "That way." He pointed with his flash. "And don't try anything, all right? I got nothing against either one of you. But I'll sure as hell shoot if I have to. There's just too much riding on this."

"How did you—how did you find us?" Glenda demanded.

Stoire's voice was maddeningly calm in their

headsets. "When I first looked at your photograph, you reminded me of someone," he said. "I could not think who, although I have an excellent memory for faces. It concerned me sufficiently that I made a careful study of your dossier. An intriguing document. Carefully done. Really good work. But a few minor discrepancies. Your medical profile shows excellent physical condition, perfect teeth. Is that usual for foundlings? I do not think so. And the education you claim in your dossier does not match the abilities you showed aboard *Wayfarer*. A few other such things, all minor in themselves, but enough to make me think again. Where had I seen a blond woman who frightened me? And then I remembered. I met your mother many years ago, at least thirty years. She was blond then and was not so shy of having her photograph taken. A remarkably lovely woman, your mother. And you very much resembled the way she looked in the days before she married your father."

"Down there," Hal said. "Take that trail. And go slow."

"But how did you find us?" Glenda demanded.

"Ah. Once I knew who you were, it was obvious that I would have to question your, ah, lover. Mr. Dykes was most uncooperative, but he is not security minded. There was a copy of a map, marked, in his quarters. It took no great ability to go on from there."

They reached a wide ravine and started down into it.

"I don't suppose you would like to tell me how much you have found out," Stoire said.

"Go to hell," Kevin told him.

"Be polite." Stoire's voice had a hard edge. "So far I have been as gentle as possible under the circumstances. You can be made to talk, Senecal, and you are expendable. I point out that we have more air in our tanks than you have in yours. We need only wait. For that matter, I expect you would tell us anything to spare the young lady the ordeal of our questioning—"

"Kevin, don't say anything!" Glenda shouted.

"But you see, it doesn't really matter what you know," Stoire said. "I have Dykes, and we have drugs. It will not be necessary to question you two, which is as well for you."

They reached the bottom of the ravine. There was a scooter there. "Get on," Hal said. He took wire from his tool kit and bound Kevin and Glenda to the scooter seats. "All right, sir, I can handle them," the pilot said.

"Undoubtedly," Stoire said. "But—I think I will accompany you. Miss Hansen-MacKenzie is not above offering bribes—"

"I know better," the pilot insisted.

"Of course you do. Still, I think we will both be happier if we know we can trust each other—and the ride should be entertaining." Stoire climbed onto the scooter seat. "Let's go."

XVI

The pilot came around and turned off their transmitters. He left the receivers on. "Okay, kids," he said. "Hang on." He climbed into the saddle and ignited the rocket motor. The scooter rose swiftly from Ceres. The pilot studied the plot in his navigation screen, then made careful course corrections. They moved rapidly away from Ceres, out into the black depths of space.

Kevin leaned toward Glenda. Their helmets touched. "It looks like he's taking us up to C-4," Kevin said. "That doesn't make sense."

"Kevin, we've got to get loose—"

"Sure. How?" He strained against the wire that held him. Nothing gave. "I can't do anything. And Stoire's watching—"

"I don't know what to do either."

"I love you."

"Kevin, I'm—do you really think they meant it? Where could he be taking us? I think they're going to dump us in space."

"They want you as a hostage," Kevin said. He tried to sound more confident than he felt.

And yet, he thought, it made sense. If there was a place Stoire could keep her, it could be important to have Glenda Hansen-MacKenzie on tap. MacKenzie's reputation was known all over the world. If he made a promise—or a threat—he'd keep it. What might he do to get his daughter back? But it didn't make sense to keep Kevin Senecal alive. . . .

* * *

There was a stony rock a hundred meters in diameter just ahead. It was smaller than C-4. There were signs of mining on it, but no lights or people. It looked deserted.

Donnelly carefully maneuvered the scooter toward the rock, and finally set it down. "Well, here you are," he said. "Your new home."

"Where are we?" Kevin asked.

"C-2," Stoire said. "Abandoned three thousand hours ago. There was enough equipment left here to keep you alive. Food, oxygen, fuel cells. We will take your suits and radios—"

"Do you really want to do that, sir?" Donnelly asked. "May as well kill them and be done with it. Their radios won't reach Ceres, and they will probably have to make outside repairs. If you want them alive, you'd better leave them their suits."

"All right," Stoire said.

"Of course, there aren't any scooters here," Donnelly said. He came around with a pair of wire cutters. He clipped the wires holding Kevin's left hand to the scooter, then pulled Kevin's hands together and took a turn of wire around them. Then he did the same to Glenda before he cut them free from the scooter.

"There," he said. "I'll leave your tool kits, too.

You'll get loose with a little work. The airlock's right over there. Now, off you go. Go on, jump. Move. Get going."

They jumped off the scooter.

"Careful how you wiggle around," Donnelly said. "You can jump right off this rock. Won't do you any good except to kill you, of course, but you can do it. 'Bye." He started the scooter engine.

"Au revoir," Henri Stoire said. "Actually, I expect that's a mistatement. I do not think we will meet again." The scooter moved rapidly away.

Kevin found the wire cutters in his tool kit and helped Glenda free her hands. Then she cut him loose and they went to the airlock.

"Gauges show pressure," Glenda said. "I guess we really can live here."

"Sure." Kevin cycled the lock and they went inside. "We can stay alive, but—there's just no way we're going to get off this rock! We could be here for years."

* * *

They explored their prison. There wasn't much to see. A few hundred meters of tunnels sprayed with plastic to hold air; some chambers carved out as quarters; and gear left when the mining operations were suspended.

"There's a lot of valuable stuff here," Kevin said. "Surely someone will come back for it."

"When Henri Stoire orders it done," Glenda said bitterly. "It all belongs to Interplanet."

"Yeah." Kevin continued to check the equipment available. "There's mining stuff."

"So we mine the rocks, refine steel, and build a

scooter," Glenda said. "Somehow I don't think that's going to work."

"No. I guess not." Kevin continued to wander. A small kitchen. Bathroom. "Hot showers," Kevin said bitterly. "All the comforts. And they weren't lying about food. Enough to keep us going for months. Not much variety, I'm afraid. TVP'S. Dehydrated stew. Well, we won't starve."

They wouldn't run out of power either. There were tanks of hydrogen and oxygen, and a dozen fuel cells to produce electricity from them.

There was even a thick window set in the outer room of the mine. It looked down on Ceres. The tiny rock was locked in rotation with Ceres so that it always faced the asteroid below.

"So near and so far," Kevin said. "It might as well be a million instead of three hundred kilometers." He watched as they moved over Ceres. It would be simple enough to jump off their moonlet prison, but it would do no good: they would still be in orbit around Ceres.

Kevin took out his pocket computer. "C-2. We are 284 kilometers above the surface and we're moving at not quite three-tenths of a kilometer a second relative to Ceres. That's just about a thousand kilometers an hour."

"Which might as well be a million," Glenda said. "Could we send a message? There are energy sources here, we can make a spark-gap transmitter. Send an SOS."

"And who'd hear it first?" Kevin asked. "The probability is pretty good that Stoire would get it. He controls all the communications. And the computer. And I doubt that he'd like it. Donnelly would be the logical one to send up to 'rescue' us, and then—"

"Damn. I have made a rather thorough mess of things, haven't I?"

"I'm worried about Jacob."

She nodded. "So am I. I haven't even dared think about him. Do—can they make Bill Dykes tell them that Jacob was helping us?"

"Given enough time, or the right drugs, anybody can be made to tell anything."

"And then they'll kill Bill and Jacob both." Glenda's voice was bitter and full of self-accusation. "It's my fault. I wanted to be certain. I wanted to find out where they had hidden the Arthurium. Catch all the conspirators. Give the whole package to Aeneas, all wrapped up."

"You tried to get a message off. What more could you have done?" Kevin demanded.

"I don't know. I could have tried to get help. I think Dr. Vaagts would have believed me. Or Joe Harwitt. Westinghouse has a lot to lose—"

"Not if they're buying the Arthurium. And you can't know, Glenda. With this much at stake, anybody could be involved. Anybody at all."

"I know. That's what my father warned me about before I left. He didn't want me to come—"

"I don't blame him much."

"But I had to be so damned smart! And I've gotten ten my friends killed, and there's nothing I can do. I couldn't even get a message off!"

Kevin shrugged. "We did the best we could—"

"Did we? I didn't try everything. I could have sent something through the main computer."

Kevin frowned. "I suppose Jacob could have done that. It would have been dangerous. What we tried was better. A few more hours and we'd have done it. Or if Dykes hadn't left that marked map. . . ."

"Jacob had another plan," Ellen said. "He was working on the instructions Stoire gave the computer. Jacob thinks he can take control of the main computer away from Stoire. With just a little more work. Then we'd have been in control of the whole station."

"Yeah, but it has to work the first time," Kevin said. "All they need to do is keep Norsedal away from the control console."

"They couldn't keep me away," Glenda said. "If I knew the key commands, I could make the computer obey me. I should have waited, but no, I had to do things my way. Damn, I'm an idiot."

"Don't be so hard on yourself. How could you order their computer around?"

"Implant. I have a transceiver implant, and an acceptor was put into the Ceres main computer when it was built on Earth. It was supposed to be my secret weapon, but I never got a chance to use it."

"Implant." Kevin fell silent for a moment. "I'm told those cost half a million francs."

She didn't say anything.

"I keep forgetting. You have half a million francs. A lot more. What—how does it feel to grow up rich?" he asked.

"Confined. Filled with obligations if your father is Aeneas MacKenzie."

"Yeah, I guess it would be like that."

"I ran away from it," Glenda said. "Oh, not really. But I grew up on the Moon, and I was the little princess, and it was stifling. When I was fifteen, I convinced myself I couldn't stand it any longer. I went to Earth for an education." She shuddered. "It was terrible at first. Getting used to high gravity, to rain, and dust and storms and cars and freeways—terrible and magnificent too. Sailing. I learned to sail a boat. You can fly on the Moon, but you can't sail.

"So I went to school on Earth and I had this phoney identity, and I kidded myself I was independent, but of course I wasn't. I was still taking mother's money. And I was always afraid any boys I met would find out who I was and then they'd pretend to like me because I was the little princess —I was a mess, Kevin.

"I realized that finally, that I was worse off than ever because I was taking the benefits of being a Hansen-MacKenzie and I was shucking the responsibilities. So when I went back for a visit and heard about the Ceres operation and heard mother worrying about the small yields of Arthurium, I decided it was time to try to earn my keep."

"So it was all made up, about you and the foster homes, and the Futurians?"

"Most of it. Not the Futurians. They're real, and I am a junior member of their Fellowship. I thought Aeneas would be upset about it, but he wasn't. He supports them, and they've helped us. They're one reason you're here, Kevin."

"How's that?"

"Dr. Farrington is one of the Fellowship. One of

the leaders. After—when we were on the ship, I was curious about you, so I sent for more information. One of the messages I got back was from him. He thinks highly of you."

"But—why did you want to know more about me?"

"Do I have to tell you?" She moved closer to him. "Kevin, I'm afraid I've made a thorough mess of everything. I don't feel much like Miss Supercompetent Independence just now."

"And I'm one poor excuse for a hero," Kevin said. "But I do love you—"

"And you said so before you knew who I was. That's important," she said. And then they didn't talk at all for a long time.

* * *

The scooter came back thirty hours later. It didn't land. Instead it closed to a few dozen meters from their moonlet and a suited figure leaped off. As the scooter drove away again, the newcomer landed with a suit reaction pistol and came to the airlock.

"Jacob!" They let him in eagerly. "What happened?" Kevin demanded.

"They caught me," Norsedal sighed. "And it's worse than that. They killed your friend Dykes—"

"Oh no." Tears formed in Glenda's eyes.

"And Wiley Ralston," Norsedal said.

"Wiley? How was he mixed up in this?" Kevin asked.

"He was an agent for the African bloc," Norsedal said. "Stoire had him arrested and held a trial. Accused him of murdering you two, and George

Lange. He was probably guilty of killing Lange, and he confessed to trying to kill the two of you when you were leaving Earth—"

"He was the saboteur on *Wayfarer*?" Kevin asked. "Wiley?"

"It looks that way," Jacob said. "He was executed for it."

"Damn," Kevin muttered. "There goes that chance. I was trying to see how Stoire intended to get away with it. I mean, the Hansen-MacKenzie heir can't just vanish! Aeneas MacKenzie would be out here with a shipload of Hansen security agents and blood in his eye—"

"And now he's got a scapegoat," Glenda said. "Dad will be suspicious, but—is there any evidence left?"

"There is now," Jacob said. "The computer still has a record of what happened. But Stoire will have done something about that before Mr. MacKenzie arrives. He is coming, by the way. There was a report that *Valkyrie* left Luna Station seven hundred hours ago. I wouldn't be surprised if he were bringing company police. But you've been reported dead and your murderer has been caught and executed."

"Looks pretty hopeless," Kevin said. "Unless you brought along a pocket scooter."

"Alas, no," Norsedal said. "They even took my computer."

"I don't understand why you're alive," Kevin said.

Jacob grinned slightly. "They're having some problems with the main computer just now. If they ever get them fixed, I'll be expendable, but they thought it might be best to have me around just in case they don't find the bugs."

"Will that stop them?" Glenda asked.

"Alas, no. Mr. Stoire is very clever. He'll figure out what I did, just as I finally figured out what he did."

"You know, then?" Kevin asked.

"Yes. Could I have some water?"

"Sure. There's plenty. Plenty of everything. We could be here for years," Kevin said.

"Not me." Norsedal's voice didn't change. "You see, they didn't leave me any insulin."

"How—how long?" Glenda asked after a while.

"If I'm careful about what I eat, three or four hundred hours," Jacob said. "Perhaps longer."

"We've got to get out of here," Glenda said.

"I agree, but I confess I don't know how," Norsedal said. "I was telling you what Stoire did. It was very clever, really. First he programmed the computer to report a much lower percentage of Arthurium in the ore. Understand, the computer knew better, and the refinery operated just the same as it always did, but the reported recovery was low. They they told the computer to forget about one storage area, and routed ninety percent of the Arthurium there. Simple, clean, and really very pretty. And once Stoire erases the real log, there'll be no record of it at all."

* * *

They had explored every tunnel in the prison a dozen times, but found nothing. A hundred hours passed.

There was nothing they could do. No laser equipment to send signals with. No electronics. Nothing but some mining gear and the basic materials for staying alive. Even that took a lot of work. The algae in the tank farms had died, and their own power source was fuel cells. There were tanks of hydrogen and oxygen for those, but the carbon dioxide scrubbers needed constant recharging. They had less time than Kevin had thought.

"I would say two people have a thousand hours more oxygen," Norsedal said. "I could—" He hesitated. "I can add a couple of hundred hours to that, and it won't really matter."

"I'll be damned if you will," Kevin said. "Something will turn up."

"I doubt it," Jacob said. "C-4 is scheduled to go in about nine hundred hours. Daedalus is putting in the final equipment right now."

"And then Stoire and Donnelly are gone," Kevin said. "But how does he get away with it?"

Jacob shrugged. "It would be no great trick to put the Arthurium aboard C-4. As gold, for example. The bombs go off, C-4 heads for Earth. Somewhere between here and there a ship—it wouldn't have to be a very large one—meets them and when C-4 arrives in Earth orbit, the Arthurium is gone, with nothing left aboard that's not supposed to be there."

"And it was stupid to leave us alive," Kevin said. "Once he's ready to leave, he'll come back with Donnelly and finish us. No evidence, no embarrassing bodies—"

"More likely he will take Glenda on C-4," Jacob

said. "Donnelly is part of his crew."

"I'm going to go have another look around," Kevin said. "There's got to be *something* we can do."

"I hope you think of it," Glenda said. "I can't."

"Alas, nor I," Jacob added.

* * *

Kevin prowled through the corridors of their prison. There has to be some way, he told himself. Ceres mocked him from below, less than three hundred kilometers down. It hung huge in the night sky.

Three hundred kilometers down, and we're moving about half a kilometer a second relative to Ceres, Kevin thought. That's not very much velocity. Under a thousand miles an hour. It doesn't take much energy to get to that speed. How much gasoline does it take to accelerate a car on Earth up to a hundred miles an hour—a gallon or so? We only need ten times that, not even that much.

There's plenty of hydrogen and oxygen. Marvelous rocket fuels if we only had a rocket. More than enough to get us down, except that the temperature of hydrogen burning in oxygen is a lot hotter than anything we have to contain in it—

No. That's not right. The fuel cells do it. But they do it by slowing down the reaction, and they can't be turned into rocket engines.

He remembered the early German Rocket Society experiments described by Willy Ley. The Berliners had blown up more rockets than they flew, and they were only using gasoline, not hydrogen. Liquid-fuel rockets need big hairy pumps, and

Kevin didn't have any pumps.

What did he have? Fuel cells, plenty of them, and so what? An electric-powered rocket was theoretically possible, but Kevin didn't have the faintest idea of how to build one, even if there was enough equipment around to do it with. He wasn't sure anyone had ever built one—certainly he couldn't.

Back to first principles, he thought. The only way to change velocity in space is with a rocket. What is a rocket? A machine for throwing mass overboard. The faster the mass thrown away goes in one direction, the faster the rocket will go in the other, and the less you have to throw. All rockets are no more than a means of spewing out mass in a narrow direction. A rocket could consist of a man sitting in a bucket and throwing rocks backward.

That might get a few feet per second velocity change, but so what? There simply wasn't enough power in human muscles—even if he did have a lot of rocks. Was there any other way to throw them? Not fast; and unless the thrown-away mass had a high velocity, the rocket wouldn't be any use. He went on through the tunnels, looking at each piece of equipment he found, trying to think of how it might be used.

You can throw *anything* overboard to make a rocket. Hydrogen, for example. That's all *Wayfarer*'s engines did, heat up hydrogen and let it go out through the rocket nozzle. We have hydrogen under pressure—

Not enough. Nowhere near enough hydrogen

and nowhere near enough pressure, not to get velocity changes of hundreds of miles an hour. Ditto for oxygen. Gas under compression just can't furnish enough energy. What would? Chemical energy; burning hydrogen in oxygen would do it, but it gave off too much; there was nothing to contain that reaction except the fuel cells and they did it by slowing the reaction way down and—

And I'm back where I started, Kevin thought. Plenty of energy in the fuel cells if I could find a way to use it. Could I heat a gas with electricity? Certainly, only how—

His eye fell on the hot-water tank in the crew quarters. An electric hot-water tank. There was a pressure gauge: forty pounds per square inch. Forty p.s.i.—He looked at the tank as if seeing it for the first time, then went running back to the others.

"Glenda, Jacob, I've got it."

XVII

Jacob Norsedal bent over Kevin's pocket calculator. "I have worked it by three different methods and I get nearly the same answer each way," he said. "I believe it will work."

"Sure it works." Kevin grinned. "Steam at forty p.s.i. will come out *fast*. About a kilometer a second."

"I believe you," Glenda said. "But it sounds silly. *Steam* rockets?"

Kevin shrugged. "It is silly. There are a lot more efficient systems. But this will work—"

"In a low g field," Jacob said. "You will not have much thrust. Of course you won't need much."

"I'm sure it works," Kevin said. "Now all we have to do is build it." He made himself sound confident; he knew how much room for error there was in his figures. "Look, it takes 980 calories to turn a gram of water into steam. We heat that steam up another thirty or forty degrees and let it out. The energy is moving molecules. We know the molecular weight of water, so we can figure the number of molecules in a gram and—"

"I worked it too," Glenda reminded him. "And

I get the same answer you do, but it doesn't mean I trust it."

"What else can we do?" Kevin asked.

"Nothing. You're right. Let's get to work."

* * *

They disconnected the hot-water tank and drilled holes in it. Several turns of heating wire went through the holes, then they sealed them in with epoxy. At one end of the tank they drilled a large hole and threaded a pipe into it, threaded a large valve onto the pipe, and welded a makeshift rocket nozzle beyond that.

When it was done they tethered the tank and filled it with water, then connected a fuel cell to the heating leads. "Here goes," Kevin said. He threw the switch to start the heaters.

Slowly the water inside heated, then began to boil. The pressure shown on the gauge began to rise. In half an hour they had forty-five pounds of pressure. "All right, let's try it," Kevin said.

Glenda turned the valve to let out steam. A jet of steam and water shot out across the surface of the moonlet. Ice crystals formed in space and slowly settled to the rocket surface. The jet reached far away from them, well off the moonlet itself. The tank pulled against its tether lines, stretching the rope.

"It works!" Kevin shouted. "Damn it, we're going to make it!" He shut off the electricity. "Let's get her finished."

* * *

It didn't look like a spaceship. It didn't even resemble a scooter, crude as those were. It looked like a hot-water tank with fuel cells bolted onto it. For controls it had vanes set crosswise in the exhaust stream, spring-loaded to center, with two tillers, one for each vane; a valve to control steam flow; and switches to connect the fuel cells to the heaters. Nothing else.

The tank itself was fuzzy: They'd sprayed it with styrofoam, building it up in layers until they had nearly a foot of insulation. There were straps on opposite sides of the tank to hold two passengers on.

The tank held nearly a hundred gallons of water. Kevin calculated that they had more than enough energy to boil it all in their two fuel cells, and they would only need sixty gallons to get to Ceres. The number was so small that he ran it four times, but it was correct.

The strangest part was the stability system: a pair of wheels taken from a mining cart and set up in front of the water tank. Electric motors rotated the wheels in opposite directions.

"Damndest gyros in the history of space research," Kevin said when they got the ship completed. "In fact, it's the damndest rocket ever."

"It ought to have a name," Glenda said. "Something heroic, fitting a knight rescuing us from durance vile—"

"How about Fudgesicle?" Kevin suggested.

"You'll hurt its feelings," Glenda said.

"The Gump?" Norsedal asked apologetically.

"Stop that! *Galahad.* That will do nicely, I think."

"You're crazy," Kevin said.

Norsedal laughed. Glenda's own laugh was strained. "I'm about to get aboard that thing, and you say I'm crazy? And you built it? Kevin, are we ready?"

"I guess so. I've been putting off the awful moment, but—"

"Right. Come on, Jacob—"

Norsedal sighed. "I have been over the calculations. That Gump *cannot* carry three people. You will be lucky to get down alive with two. Therefore I am not coming."

"You have to!" Glenda insisted. "If you don't get down, it does us no good—"

"Not true," Norsedal said. "I've given you the key words. And you do not know where you will land. Now it's true that I get around better in low gravity than I ever did on Earth, but it is also true that I am not athletic. I doubt that I can make my way over hundreds of kilometers of ravines—not in my present condition."

"You're feeling the lack of insulin?" Kevin demanded.

"Yes," Norsedal sighed.

"One of us should stay with you—" Glenda said. She sounded doubtful.

"Nonsense. You must go, because Kevin could do nothing alone once he gets there. Kevin should go because it is more likely I will be rescued if you two get down safely, and two are more likely to succeed than one. Now, are you ready?"

"I guess so," Kevin said.

"Then let's do it before we lose our nerve," Glenda said.

"Right." The total mass of *Galahad* with full water tank was just under .550 kilograms. In C-2's tiny gravity it was no problem at all to carry it outside.

They stood on the rocky surface of the moonlet to let their eyes adjust to starlight. Ceres filled a full sixty degrees below them, a third of space, so close they could not even see all of it. It loomed huge and darkly forbidding, its surface lit by sunlight to a brightness much less than Earth's moon, but it was enormously larger than any full moon.

"We won't have any trouble finding it," Kevin said.

"No," Norsedal said. "But finding it is not your main problem."

"Don't I know it."

Glenda said nothing. All three of them had tried to work the problem of a landing orbit, and they couldn't do it with a pocket calculator. The equations for low-thrust trajectories were too complex, and they had too little data about *Galahad's* probable performance. They would simply have to navigate by eye and hope to cancel out all their velocities.

They carried the hot-water tank to a low peak on the moonlet and pointed it so that the rocket nozzle was aimed as close to the direction they moved across Ceres's face as they could manage.

"Time," Kevin said.

"I'm scared—"

"I'm terrified," Kevin said. "But what choices have we? You know damned well Stoire and Donnelly will be back—"

"Yes. Let's do it."

It took only a gentle effort to push the steam rocket away from the moonlet, but the cartwheel-gyros resisted any effort to turn it. Finally they got it oriented properly in space. Then they climbed aboard.

"Full head of steam," Kevin said. "Almost fifty pounds. Ready?"

"Ready—"

He twisted the steam valve. At first both steam and water were expelled from the tank, but as they began to accelerate, the water settled and the exhaust valve let out only steam. C-2 dropped away. They missed it. It was a prison, but a safe one; now they had only their makeshift steam rocket.

Galahad showed a tendency to tumble, but with the gyros resisting, they were able to control it with the steering vanes. A plume of steam shot from the tank, rapidly crystallizing into ice fog that engulfed them.

"Damn. That's going to make it hard to see," Kevin said. "Nothing we can do about it." He peered down toward Ceres. It didn't seem any closer. Jacob's farewell faded in their headsets.

Norsedal's calculations had shown that twenty minutes' thrust should be enough to cancel all their orbital velocity. It would use up just about half their fuel. Once *Galahad* was stopped dead in orbit above Ceres, they would fall toward the asteroid, and they would have half their steam left to counteract that.

The trouble was that Jacob couldn't calculate how high above Ceres they would be when the twenty minutes were finished. As they lost velocity, they would lose altitude, and their orbit would no longer be a smooth circle, but an ellipse intersecting Ceres—somewhere. At the end of twenty minutes Kevin cut the power off. He was pleased that they still had thirty pounds of steam pressure.

After half an hour they were noticeably closer to the asteroid. It was time to start the steam again. They had to change direction of thrust many times, using the steering vanes to turn the tank. It was easy to over-correct and they wasted steam in swaying back and forth hunting for the correct orientation. Mostly, though, there was nothing to do but wait and hope.

As they came closer, they could see details on the craggy surface below. Rugged canyons, high peaks, deep valleys, and rocks everywhere. Kevin had a protractor which he used to measure the angle Ceres filled in the space below them. Then he used that to calculate their altitude. It was crude and certainly not accurate to better than ten percent, but it was all they had.

"I read a hundred degrees," Kevin said. "That puts us just about a hundred kilometers above Ceres. If I've figured everything right, and if I'm reading the angles right—"

"You have to be right, don't you?" Glenda said. "There's nothing else we can do."

She was right. They couldn't get back to C-2 now, and they wouldn't be able to find the tiny moonlet even if they had the reaction mass.

"Time for another turn," Kevin said. "I think."

"We're still moving—"

"Yes, but that's what the numbers say."

"All right."

And a year ago I was working equations in school, Kevin thought. Numbers to crunch and write down for examinations. Now they're something to stake your life on. He twisted the tiller slightly. The tank rotated, and he pointed the tiller the other way to stop it. It took several more adjustments before he thought he had it right. Now the steam jet pointed almost directly toward Ceres, counteracting the asteroid's pull.

He was tempted to change the steam flow, but he didn't dare. That was the part he couldn't calculate at all. The mass of their tank changed constantly as steam spewed out, and as the mass fell, the thrust increased. If they turned the steam valve up too high, it would more than counteract Ceres's gravity, and they would move away from it; and when they ran out of steam, they would fall again, this time with no stopping, impacting at seven or eight hundred miles an hour.

"I feel like singing," Kevin shouted. "I am I, Don Quixote, the Lord of La Mancha, my destiny calls and I go—"

"Which makes me Rosalinda, the scullery maid?" Glenda demanded.

"You would rather be Sancho Panza? —No, that's Jacob. And *Galahad* is our charger. Now I need a broken lance and a bent sword—"

"I think we're getting closer."

"So do I." Kevin took out his protractor and eyeballed the size of Ceres below. They could no longer see much of the asteroid; they were low enough that there was a definite horizon less than 150 kilometers to each side. "When we get closer, we have to kill our velocity relative to the ground. Otherwise the landing impact will kill us."

"Where will we hit . . . I mean land?"

"I don't know. Fifty, seventy-five kilometers from the station, I hope. We brought plenty of spare air tanks."

For a long time they had seemed to be falling very slowly. Now, as they got closer, they seemed to be moving faster. Much too fast. Kevin couldn't estimate their speed, but it was many meters per second. He used the tillers to turn *Galahad* directly toward Ceres, opened the steam valve wider.

Not too wide, he told himself. Not too wide, or we'll use up steam too fast and—

The temptation to blast as hard as they could was almost irresistible. The craggy ground came up toward them at frightening speed. They were definitely coming down too fast, and they were too close. Desperately he opened the steam valve all the way, and switched full power to the heaters—

A minute went by. Another. Now they were very low—and they didn't seem to have much approach velocity, but they were moving across the surface much too quickly. Painfully they rotated the tank until the exhaust pointed in the direction they moved over the ground, then tilted it again toward Ceres. Kevin opened the steam valve again.

"We've still got pressure," he said. "But I have no idea how much water is left in the tank—"

"Don't talk about it," Glenda said grimly. "We're so close—"

"Sure." Now they were less than a kilometer high, still moving too fast. Again Kevin rotated toward Ceres, ignoring their lateral velocity to kill their falling speed. "Keep a lookout for large objects in our path—"

"I'd say we're moving fifty miles an hour," Glenda said.

"Enough to kill you—" But slowly the rocket lost velocity toward the ground, and they were able to turn again. "Pick a landing site," Kevin said. "Something under our ground track."

"Over there. Ahead of us." He looked quickly toward the plateau she had selected. It was rocky but as good as anything else in sight. He rotated the rocket again; they were moving slantwise toward the ground, and Kevin kept the exhaust pointing straight in their direction of travel.

The steam pressure was falling. They were running out of water, or else they were using steam faster than the fuel cells could boil the water; it didn't matter. A few more seconds and they'd be down, one way or another—

The plateau came up toward them, but not so fast now. The steam valve was wide open. Nothing else they could do.

They were over the plateau and falling directly toward it, a hundred meters high and falling—plummeting straight down.

"Cut loose from the straps," Kevin shouted. "Be ready to jump clear just before we hit."

He worked frantically at the buckles, but he couldn't unfasten them and keep control of the tillers. The rocket showed a definite tendency to tumble now as Glenda moved in her perch, but there wasn't time for more talk, for more of anything—

Fifty meters. Twenty-five. Slowing all the time. Maybe they'd make it after all—

Then the ground came up and swatted them. They hit tail first. The rocket nozzle collapsed beneath, and steam spewed out, forming an ice fog that condensed on the rocks and on his face plate. He worked at the buckles and got them loose—

And realized he was lying on the surface. He couldn't see, but he heard Glenda's voice in his helmet. "Kevin! Are you all right?"

She didn't sound hurt. Gingerly he worked each limb. Nothing seemed broken. "We're down," he said.

Kevin estimated their landing velocity at about ten miles an hour. The crumpled rocket nozzle had absorbed much of the energy of the crash, and neither of them had been more than shaken up. "Any landing you walk away from is a good one," Kevin remembered a pilot had once told him. "Donnelly—"

"What?"

"Nothing. Something Donnelly told me once. When we were still friends. Glenda, I haven't the faintest idea of where we are."

"Sure you do. Why do you think we have visibility even though we're on the night side?" She pointed up at the bright disc above them. "The station is just under the synchronous mirror."

"Yeah. I'm not thinking too well—"

"You're doing all right." She pointed to the remains of their steam rocket. "Splendidly, I'd say."

They loaded up all the full oxygen tanks and set out toward the satellite mirror. Kevin stopped to take an observation with his protractor, then punched numbers into his calculator. "I make it ninety to a hundred kilometers," he said.

"Not too bad. A few hours of following yonder star. We've got enough air."

"If we don't use it up talking." Kevin started bounding across the surface of the asteroid. Glenda followed.

They moved in long leaps. It was much easier than walking, almost like ice skating or skipping down hill; as long as they could keep going in a straight line, it took very little effort. Turning or stopping was much harder.

They could leap crevasses up to forty meters wide, and it was easy enough to go around bigger ones. If they had to climb, they could jump thirty meters upward, or jump down steep slopes.

It was like a combination of flying and skating, leaping across the surface of Ceres, and Kevin shouted with the sheer joy of being alive. They *were* alive, and for a while they were safe.

In seven hours they were within sight of Ceres Station. They paused on a hilltop looking down on the leveled plain which served as the spaceport.

"We could try to steal one of the scooters," Kevin said. "I think we can trust John Eliot and the Daedalus people."

"Except that the scooters are guarded, and our best chance is the plan we already worked out. *Everyone* on Ceres can't be corrupt. Most of the people here believe in the future of the Belt—"

"All right," Kevin said. "Let's go."

They went directly to the main entrance to the station. There was no one in the airlock, and once inside, they went into Fat Jack's bar.

* * *

The bar was crowded with people singing and shouting. One by one they fell silent as they stared at Kevin and Glenda.

"You're dead," Joe Harwitt said. "Damn it, Bill Dykes said you were dead! He said you'd been killed by Ralston!"

"Did he say it to you?" Glenda asked. "Or to Henri Stoire and Hal Donnelly?"

There was a short silence. Then one of the miners said, "Hell, Stoire and Donnelly were the only ones with Bill when he died. You saying they lied to us?"

"Damn right," Kevin said. "They're the ones who marooned us on C-2."

"On C-2?" Joe Harwitt seemed to have difficulty comprehending that. "C-2?"

"Yes. Jacob is still up there."

"He's supposed to be dead, too," one of the miners said. "Supposed to have had some kind of fight with you, Senecal. What the hell's going on here?"

"Henri Stoire is stealing Interplanet blind," Kevin said.

"We'll find out about that," another miner said. "He's coming now."

Stoire came in with four armed company police. "What is happening—Miss MacMillan! We were told you were dead."

"Good act, Stoire, but it won't work," Kevin said.

"Have you gone mad?" Stoire asked. "What are you talking about?"

"He claims you've been doing some embezzling," Joe Harwitt said.

"And what have I been stealing?" Stoire asked.

"Arthurium," Kevin said.

"Nonsense. All the Arthurium is accounted for. Six thousand, seven hundred and nine grams. No great amount, but more than has ever been seen on Earth—"

"It won't work," Glenda said. "I know precisely how much Arthurium was mined. Almost four hundred kilograms. And I know where it is."

"Ridiculous," Stoire said. "Young lady, I am trying to be patient with you and your impetuous friend, but it is obvious that you must be restrained for your own good." He turned to the others. "I don't know what she wants, but I do not have to listen to accusations from a common prostitute. Lieutenant, arrest those two."

"Yes, sir." The company police stepped forward.

"I'm no prostitute," Glenda said. "You know who I am, Mr. Stoire."

"Who?" Joe Harwitt demanded.

"I think I'll let someone else tell you," Glenda said. She looked at Stoire. "Does this mean anything to you? Balaclava, 17 September, 1976."

Stoire suddenly looked worried.

Glenda smiled faintly. "That's the code phrase he used in his secret transactions with the company's computer. Without it the computer won't deliver the full records. Jacob Norsedal figured it out from the machine language. And now—" She was quiet for a moment, a look of concentration on her face.

"HER NAME IS GLENDA HANSEN-MACKENZIE," the overhead speaker said.

"How the hell is she controlling your computer, Mr. Stoire?" one of the miners asked.

"Implant," Joe Harwitt said. "A rich young lady indeed. Only I never knew the computer could accept instructions from implants."

"Done in Zurich," Kevin said.

"Where is the missing Arthurium?" Glenda said aloud.

"I DO NOT HAVE THAT INFORMATION."

Stoire looked smug.

"How much was refined?" Glenda asked.

"THREE HUNDRED AND NINETY-TWO THOUSAND GRAMS."

"Four hundred kilos!" Joe Harwitt whistled. "Is there that much money in the whole solar system?"

"Enough that each one here can have one million francs," Henri Stoire said. "One million for each of you, if you help me."

"Jeez, that's a lot of money," someone said.

"Where will you spend it?" Glenda asked. "I have already had the base computer send a message to Hansen headquarters on Luna. You shouldn't have 'fixed' the high-gain antenna, Stoire."

"Wait a minute." Harwitt looked from Glenda to Stoire. "I don't know what to make of this. You're saying that you are Laurie Jo Hansen's kid—"

"Hell, she is," Fat Jack said. The bar owner launched himself in a smooth curve that took him next to Glenda. He looked at her intently.

"Yep. I worked for Hansen Enterprises, twenty, twenty-five years ago now. She looks like the big boss did back then. Same eyes. Yeah, I think she is."

"Where is the Arthurium?" she demanded.

Stoire shrugged. "It appears that you know something I do not. I never knew there was any more."

"You're a liar," Kevin said.

Stoire shrugged. He turned to Glenda. "I really suggest that we go somewhere and talk quietly."

"Out here." She led the way to the corridor. Kevin and the others followed. The company police looked to someone, anyone, for orders.

Glenda and Stoire moved away from the crowd. Kevin was just close enough to hear.

"It really is simple," Stoire said. "If no excess Arthurium is ever found, there is no real evidence of any crime—"

"Kidnapping—"

He shrugged again. "Possibly. But the question is, do you want your superconductors? Because if any harm comes to me, you'll never see that Arthurium again."

"It's on C-4; we'll find it." Kevin said.

"Of course," Stoire said. "With a hydrogen bomb next to it. I doubt your superconductor would be much use after it is vaporized by a one-megaton bomb."

"You're bluffing," Kevin said.

Stoire smiled thinly. "You have reason to know I believe in insurance. This is another form. Now—shall we negotiate?"

213

XVIII

The H-bomb went off in silence. A bright flower of intolerable blue-white, dying to a dull red glow.

"Just off center," Jacob Norsedal said. He looked at the computer read-out. "They'll have no trouble correcting the slight tumble. The next detonation will go off on schedule."

Aeneas MacKenzie nodded. "So C-4 is on its way. I'm surprised you didn't go with them, Jacob."

Norsedal laughed. "Three's a crowd. Newlyweds don't need company, and they can certainly manage the navigation."

"Yes. I suppose they can," MacKenzie said. He glanced at the wreckage of *Galahad*. It hadn't been easy to find, but he'd offered ten thousand francs to the miner who could locate it. Laurie Jo would want to see it—and so had he. He still couldn't believe it had worked.

"Ingenious young man, my son-in-law," MacKenzie said.

"I've reason to know it," Norsedal said. "What will happen to Stoire?"

MacKenzie shook his head. "We'll pay his debts and send him home. I doubt he'll stay away from the gaming tables long."

"It seems a shame that he gets off so easily," Norsedal said.

MacKenzie's voice was gruff. "Bill Dykes was a good friend. I don't like it much that Stoire gets off, but I doubt Bill would have wanted to pay the price for vengeance. It would have been high."

"Yes," Norsedal said. "He had the entire cargo ready to blow. Arthurium, gold, all the refined metals—"

"And not even my wife could have put more money into space without some return," MacKenzie finished. "Yes. Glenda made the only deal possible. The human race advances, but sometimes we pay in strange coin, Jacob."

"Time," Norsedal said. The viewscreen flared again, a point of brilliant white fading rapidly. Norsedal studied the radar returns. "Well done," he said. He watched the computer read-out a moment longer, then looked up. "Will you be staying long?"

"No. I'm taking the Arthurium back to Luna in *Valkyrie*. We can be back months before C-4 arrives, and our fusion people are anxious to get to work. They think they may have a demonstration reactor by the time the kids arrive."

Norsedal typed inputs. The viewscreen blurred, then showed a map of the solar system and C-4's orbit from Ceres to Earth. "FOUR HUNDRED AND THREE DAYS," it announced.

"A long trip," Aeneas said.

"I doubt they'll notice." Norsedal's grin was wide.

Aeneas MacKenzie looked wistfully at the viewscreen. "Laurie Jo and I once had sixty days to ourselves. Sixty days with nothing to do but get to know each other. I think you're right, Jacob. They'll find this a short trip."

Norsedal grinned slightly and typed again.

"PROGNOSIS CONFIRMED," the computer announced.

There are a lot more
where this one came from!

ORDER your FREE catalog of ACE paperbacks here. We have hundreds of inexpensive
books where this one came from priced from
75¢ to $2.50. Now you can read all the books
you have always wanted to at tremendous
savings. Order your *free* catalog of ACE
paperbacks now.

ACE BOOKS ● Box 576, Times Square Station ● New York, N.Y. 10036